WordThreads' First Prose Venture

WordThreads Authors: WordThreadsAuthors@gmail.com

ISBN: 9798870392332.

First Edition, November 2023.

Printed in the United States of America

Bookman Old Style, is a serif typeface. A wide, legible design that is slightly bolder than most body text faces.

To Maggie

Contents

SPIRITUAL AND ESOTERIC

HOLY DAYS AND HOLY THOUGHTS

Nature and Animals

1   Out of the Oak – Maggie Bannister

Deep in the undergrowth, she stirs, lifts her head, takes a breath. A cool, life-giving breath, inhaling the green, feeling the life, energising her ancient limbs. She pushes upwards, sitting up, caressing the roots that have held her safe for thousands of years. It is time.

It is time to wake up.

It is time to restore the earth and bring her back to her rightful place.

It is time to allow the trees to speak and nature to sing itself to fullness.

Her hair is a mass of brambles forming dark curls around her strong features. From her mouth spring shoots searching for light, eager for warmth, spreading around her face. Oak leaves are her headdress. Acorns nestled in decoration. She is beautiful, dark, earthy, full of potential. Her eyes flecked with gold and green, searching carefully for signs of life.

She looks up, into the canopy already forming, green shoots bursting from branches high above, into the abundant life of the forest. She closes her eyes and listens, lifting her head to the warmth of the sun.

Long has she waited, at rest within the depths of the oak. When she went to sleep this tree was not yet born, and yet it has been her resting place for many centuries. She has lain under the earth, dreaming of ancient ways and sensuous encounters.

The old oak has awakened her from her sleep, calling in desperation for her help.

For the forest, this ancient soft, breathing, damp and fertile home, needs her again.

'Come' says the mossy bed around her. 'Come and walk again. Come and weave your magic. Bring life into our roots. Call the rain to fall, to nourish us.'

'Come', says the stream. 'Come and cleanse us, fill our waters with fish, and play in our path.'

'Come', say the birds. 'Come and save our nests, breathe on the plants for our food, hold our fledglings in your tendrils.'

'Come' say the trees. Come and shelter in our shade, wrap yourself around our living branches. Keep us from harm.'

The Green Woman opened her eyes. It was too late. The axe fell.

2   Black Kitten – Anila Syed

Getting used to an amazing new smell is the first test. That umami marmite spread around the living room air. Only a mother could love.

Visitors wrinkle their noses – polite ones. Everyone else just asks: Is that your kitten farting?

Yes, I volunteer, shoulders permanently shrugging.

My atmosphere is generously lubricated with a mixture of milk and cat food, liberally fermented for a few hours in kitten intestine.

I open a french window, just a crack. A little black nose sits there for an hour, breathing the outside. She looks at me with her quick darting graze of a gaze, as if I am the source of the smell.

It's not me, buster.

Buster.

OK, Buster the little black girl kitten, it is.

The kittenette.

The black streak of a mad half hour every day, toppling my carefully balanced stacks of books as if she is a living computer-game kitten. A hundred points for a stack of five. Five hundred to scatter today's post around the house.

The black hole of gravity which pins me down for the rest of the time, finding me to be the most comfortable spot in the world to sleep away some vital hours of regeneration. A little kitten time lord.

The children make a dangly, jingly thing which focuses the mad half hour, even when there is no-one to dangle or jingle it.

I take up 12 megabytes, trying to get a picture of her without blur, or furry monster close-up peering right down the lens, or brightly-lit shining devil eyes.

She stares intently as I type. Finding the laptop forever the place de rigeur. Too many emails of gibberish whisk around the world before I get a chance to close the lid.

She looks at me, affronted, pinning me down, holding my face in her paws. 'You can't do that. I was busy.' I hear. 'How do you think Grumpy Cat got started?'

I open the lid for her and she is once again pouncing on something.

I make a YouTube channel for her: Pouncy kitten.

We spend our days in symbiosis, sharing our on-line existence. She suffers me to type my work, forever guarding my lap or my face, or my head. When it is her turn, she comes and sits across my typing fingers, her yellow saucer smile enough to say, 'Me now'.

I am a cat now. Frenzied activity is all I'm allowed during the morning. The rest of the day I am an accessory. A plaything for a kitten. She loves to cling.

She digs her claws in at any sign of resistance, gazing deeply into my eyes, her eyes narrowed in a smile.

It is definitely a smile. I look it up on Buzzfeed: 10 ways your cat is trying to kill you.

'Not that one,' I hear. She jumps around the keyboard.

25 signs your cat really loves you.

Aw! Thanks Buster.

She sits on me, smiling, hypnotising me.

I can't sit here forever. I want a cup of tea.

'OK, get your tea,' she thinks.

A hot cup of tea is in my hand, steam swirling lazily.

"There."

"Well, thanks!"

"Anything else?"

"No – Yes – Why can I hear you?"

She looks away, blinking. I must have fallen asleep. I thought...haha, never mind what I thought.

I watch her for a few days. Any remarks of hers flying my way? I try to capture fuzzy stray wisps of kitten thought. Nothing.

She catches me, staring intently at the back of her head and stands up suddenly to show me a puckered little bottom. OK, OK, I get the message.

But why did you speak to me and why have you stopped? How can I magic more tea?

I get two minutes of work done before she pins me down, sitting on my chest. Little, perfectly formed, cuddly toy paws resting on my chin. Her eyes are deep. They are green now? No, it's her pupils, expanded beyond all reason. She is drawing me in. The laptop whirs. Its keys are humming and soft, springy. Just right for a pouncy kitten.

'Can you hear me?' I think, gazing deeply into those cavern eyes.

"You're changing."

"What? I'm not changing."

"No, it's a good thing."

That smile.

Eyes narrowed, pointy little furry face both dreaming and intense.

10 ways your cat is trying to kill you?

"No! Not at all!"

"What then?"

She shifts her weight slightly on my laptop keyboard.

One more calculating stare. One tiny smile. She stands up, stretches luxuriously and jumps.

I gasp.

I'm staring at the screen.

One word is large and typed in Times New Roman at the top of my new blank page.

I look for Buster, but her tail is already disappearing round the door.

The word is accusing me, or praising, or appraising me.

As soon as I see it, I feel it is right. There is a surge. A rush of overwhelming.

I look at the letters and take them in:

Witch.

A cup of tea appears in my right hand. The steam swirling lazily.

3   The Rogue Potato – Maggie Bannister

My daughter, Clare found a potato in a bag of compost in her garden, and sent me a photo of it with the title 'Rogue Potato." I couldn't resist.

Eustace didn't care one bit. He was a bad egg, his grandma told him when he was knee high to a mosquito, which was, he mused, stupid because he was a potato and nothing like an egg. He was a naughty little potato, designed for the compost bin. He refused to grow at the right time or in the right place and when Clare tipped the soil out there he was. A rogue potato.

He knew he was rather good-looking and would be able to get away with murder.

In his youth, he had cheated at snail-racing, stole his sister's eye makeup, and threw snail shells at the tomatoes, so that they fell to the ground in a huff well before they were ripe, and shrivelled to nothing. He was bored. He didn't want to grow up to be baked potato, or rösti. (Chips were only a guilty secret in his part of town).

Instead of hanging on to his mother, he set off on his own. He broke away from his family and sidled off to a far corner of the vegetable plot, taking his bag of snail shells with him, thrown over his shoulder. He had marked the bundle in snail slime to read "SLAG." – he couldn't spell very well, having spent his lessons flicking ants' eggs onto the other baby potatoes instead of paying attention.

In that corner of the bed, he learned the dark arts from beetles and cockroaches, as he began to grow. He soon craved freedom, though, and one day worked his way to the surface and hopped onto the tail of a passing fox, still carrying his bag, and wearing a fetching striped jumper and eye mask, lest his relatives saw him and dragged him down to their depths again.

He moved quickly, knowing that he should keep out of the light. He didn't want to turn green and be thrown onto the compost heap, where rats would nibble him and worms poke him. As the fox passed the tomato bed, Eustace fell off and joined his distant cousins who lived there.

But he had no sense of family loyalty. Tomatoes were just easy pickings for his mischievous ways. They hated being teased and more than that they felt far superior to potatoes. He charmed his way into their beds with flattery and then contaminated them with blight, so that they looked poor and miserable and unwanted. Eustace didn't care.

The day came – that inevitable day when someone would discover him, and when Clare found him hiding all alone, he knew his days were numbered.

He looked at Clare, blinking his pretty eyes and whispered as she picked him up, "Go on – eat me if you dare!".

So she did.

4   Capi – Patrissia Cuberos

Capi is definitely not clever; nothing seems to interest him much. I have tried politics, history, philosophy, fashion, art... name it. No interest whatsoever.

He is not good at playing games: no concept of teamwork. If I manage to get him to play with me, he loses interest almost immediately and stares at me with vacant eyes or at some non-existent point behind me.

I used to turn my head looking for that interesting something he seemed to be looking at, but I could never see anything. Perhaps he can see something I can't. Or maybe he thinks I'm an idiot, and he's got something better to do with his time.

Capi is not good at obeying orders. He always seems to have his own ideas about what I have asked him to do.

He is as messy as you get. He loves dirt, although he carries it with a certain dignity. But he definitely suffers from an eating disorder: food ends up scattered all over the place whenever he has the smallest bite.

On top of all that, Capi is a coward. The slightest noise sends him skittering to hide in the remotest corner.

However, Capi excels at one thing: he allows me to love him and responds with the same or more affection.

Although he has grown rather big, he still sits on my lap and lets me cuddle him for as long as I want; for as long as I need.

Unlike my girlfriends, he has endless patience with my clinginess and need to express affection. He never seems to fear that I will take advantage, demand sex, or that I'm trying to get something out of him.

My girlfriends always got it wrong: I don't need so much to be loved as to give love.

I believe Capi loves me. After all, he is a dog, and that's what dogs seem to do best.

Pity Capi is not a girl.

For now, Capi, I love you with all my heart for your amazing ability to let me love you without question. Bless you.

5   Tales of the Meadow – Maggie Bannister

*My neighbour has just bought the water meadow
across the road from me to turn it into a wildlife
haven. This is the beginning of the story of that
meadow from a cat's-eye point of view.*

Cobweb the cat was curious (as cats tend to be).
Something was happening in her field. Not
strictly her field, not all day anyway, but in her
mind it was HER field. Her field, her river and
her hunting ground. The old farmer, she hadn't
seen for ages, but today there were different men
in her field, wearing yellow jackets and talking
and digging little holes. She was curious and a
little cross. How could she chase the mice and
voles if men kept walking all over her patch?

She hoped they weren't going to put concrete
everywhere. That would be no good at all. No,
what she liked was plenty of tall grass to hide in,
so that she could pounce after a very long wait
(and sometimes a bit of a nap if the sun shone).
She loved the field especially as there were no
dogs, who chased her and interrupted her
meditation on the whole glorious playground that
was the field.

Cobweb had come from a farm far away,
where she could play all day with the animals.
She especially liked horses, and when she moved
she missed the horses so much. Then one day,
there were horses. She was so happy. She loved
the smell of them, their playfulness, their dignity
and their sense of humour. She wasn't a bit
scared of them. One of her favourite places to sit
was under the horse box at the end of the road,

where she could watch all the people and animals come and go. It reminded her of her very young kitten-days, when every day was a new experience, every moment a new smell, every corner a place to hide or a place to hunt.

So now she watched the men with interest. Behind her, a blackbird and a great tit were sitting side by side watching Cobweb. She was torn between chasing the birds (a waste of time as they could fly and she couldn't) as she didn't like being watched, and venturing across the bridge into her field beyond in search of voles. She had the place to herself less often these days, as two new kittens had appeared in the last few months, who were daring and agile and youthful and lived with the horses, and ran after her when she dared to be out at the same time.

Short Stories and Flashes

6   Treachery – Janet Cupit

Treachery

She had stormed out of the house, slamming the
door behind her, anger bubbling and boiling in
every fibre of her being. It was shocking beyond
belief! How could this man that she had loved for
so many years, betray her in this way. Her mind
was in turmoil.

What to do? What to do?

She forged ahead with anger powered strides
to her special place of refuge. A place of solace
and calm, where she could breathe and where the
fresh tangy breeze would ease the tightness of her
face, the beach.

It wasn't really a beach at all in the usual
sense of the word, not in this part of the country,
it was more marshland. The tight clumps of
moss and grass thriving on the coming and going
of the briny sea. Ebbing and flowing with the
tide, full of microscopic life, tiny pools of dark
water formed between the clumps of moss. The
tide didn't hurry here. It crept in quietly,
imperceptibly, insidiously. You had to be careful.

She strode on across the marshes, her
thoughts racing, oblivious to everything except
the wind and the harsh cries of the gulls, until
exhausted, she slowed and paused. An anxious
frown furrowed her brow and, filled with unease
and disquiet, she realised with alarm that she did
not know where she was; this was unfamiliar
territory.

It had become quite dark with the sun rapidly sinking below the horizon, casting a red path across the sea. Up above the stars began to appear, sharing their light across the galaxies; clear as crystal here with no light pollution. She allowed herself to embrace these wonders of nature and to take a deep sighing breath.

Impinging on her distracted consciousness, the sound of swooshing, ominous, almost silent sucking. Water dragging through roots and mud. She became aware that one foot was feeling cold and wet. With alarm she realised the tide was creeping inexorably in, making the pools deeper and darker, the clumps of moss less stable.

Don't panic! Don't panic!

Resolutely she turned her back to the sinking sun and started to stride away. Immediately her foot sank down into the cold, deep mire. Again that rush of fear and panic. She wrenched her foot free from the cloying mud and dark grim water. Test each hillock, take your time, work your way back to solid ground.

Testing and twisting, turning and testing, she became disoriented. Was she still heading in the right direction or had she turned back on herself? No landmarks on which to centre and now the sun had gone. To move or stay put? Would her family guess where she was?

They knew she would head for the sea, but she was so far from her usual favourite spot. Tears began to roll down her cheeks as her predicament became only too clear. How foolish to go stomping off in anger, instead of remaining cool and calm. Could she find the highest, firmest tuft of grass and wait out the tide? How deep did it get? Could she bear the cold and damp?

There! there, to her right she saw tiny pinpricks of light. Voices called "Mum, Mum where are you?" Relief flooded her body. She shouted, no yelled, "I'm here, I'm here, keep those lights glowing."

She wanted to run, to risk it, to get there quickly but she knew that would be foolhardy. So she started heading for those tantalising, reassuring pinpricks of hope. Testing, testing, tentatively testing, moving forwards, reaching out desperately for the achingly, sweet warm embrace of those who truly loved her.

Transcending Trauma

She had left the house, uneasy, agitated, abandoning her lunch, her mind full of dark thoughts. She needed those thoughts gone, obliterated, to feel at peace again. He had shattered her trust, her confidence, stolen her dignity. How to cope? She needed somewhere to clear her head; the beach or the moor? At the end of the road she turned left...the moor it was.

But he hadn't destroyed everything had he. She had her wonderful children, her friends, enough income to rent the small two up, two down fisherman's cottage with the sea to the front and the moor to the back, with a small wood close by. It was quiet, peaceful, idyllic.

As she turned towards the moor, the wind, storming across the moor, took her breath away and the slanting rain stung her face. She felt invigorated. She had been slightly afraid of the bleak desolation of the moorland, but now, after several months, she felt she had begun to understand this alien landscape. This place demanded respect not fear. The wind was king here; sometimes violent, turbulent, sweeping all before it; or gently stirring the cotton tops; quiet and still, allowing the birds of prey to soar on upper thermals, gliding magnificently, carefree but always with a keen eye on the world below.

The wind was strength. She could lean into it, trusting it to support her, nourish her, protect her. Deep in the hurtful memories she heard a loud snort of derision. Her fanciful, imaginative thoughts were always met with a sneer, an implied suggestion of stupidity. She had learned to keep quiet.

But no more! She could speak out, voice all the wild thoughts she wanted. She laughed out loud. Freedom. She hadn't realised. The wind captured her glee and roared with her, gradually easing to a gentle, chuckling breeze that lifted her hair and stirred the bracken.

Striding out purposefully, she headed for a small tor, a favourite spot on this moorland. Drawing near, she stepped carefully through the patch of land that had been devastated by fire during the long hot summer. For the first time she could see tiny green shoots appearing as the land recovered and replenished itself. It warmed her heart to see new life emerging. Reaching her destination, she climbed steadily to the top and sat down, sheltered by the tall upright stone that seemed to rest precariously on top of a smaller one. She always marvelled that this amazing balancing act had remained this way for hundreds of years, safe, secure, strong.

As her thoughts drifted and her body relaxed, she played with the wonderful words she had come to associate with the moor...hen harrier, Merlin, bogbean, butterworth and the fancifully named fairy shrimp pools. She could understand how people had been inspired to write fact and fiction connected to this moorland and how artists had spent hours trying to recreate the ever-changing luminosity and colours of the sky.

In the far distance she could see the sea sparkling in the sunshine, imagined she could smell and taste that tangy breeze. It was calming, quiet healing the spirit and the soul.

* * * * * * * * * *

She must have dozed, for she suddenly became aware of a coolness to the air and that the skylark had begun its lilting evening song. Time to go home...home.

Retracing her steps, she was aware of a soothing, welcome, tiredness enveloping her. The lights in the small town ahead were beginning to be switched on as evening closed in. As she turned onto her now familiar road she smiled to herself. Even though she had left home, hurriedly, anxiously she had not forgotten to place her grandmother's beautiful blue and green oil lamp (now converted to electricity) in the window, casting a warm, soft, golden light onto the garden path. A reminder that light and warmth brought reassurance and hope.

Tranquillity

She closed the door quietly behind her and smiled down at the excited, bouncy, scruffy, bundle that was her little Jack Russell dog.

She swore he knew fifteen minutes before she knew herself that she had decided on a walk. He would be at the front door, eyes sparkling, ears pricked, long tail banging against the umbrella stand.

He was her constant companion, understanding her high days and her low times. He would push his little head under her arm or rest it on her knee, soulful eyes sympathetically gazing as if to say "tell me about it."

"Where to then?" she asked the little dog. He didn't care which way she chose.

The beach meant he could run full pelt across the soft sand, barking at the waves as they crashed onto the beach, and growling at them if they dared to wet his paws.

The moor, with its breezes blowing so many different scents to be picked up by his sensitive, doggy nose.

Or the woods, where they were heading today, with its calm, ethereal light and many hidden corners for a little dog to explore. The wood was mostly birch, beech and Rowan trees, so the atmosphere was free, light and gentle, no suffocating canopy. The sunshine and the rain had easy access between the wide spreading branches, so creating a fascinating woodland floor with many different plants, ever changing with the seasons. Snowdrops, then fragrant bluebells, cow parsley, wild strawberries, aconites, so many colours and heady scents.

As they made their way to the wood, a gentle voice called "Hello my dear. It's the wood today then. A good choice." It was Mrs Trelawney, busy in her abundant garden as usual. She was a good neighbour, always helpful but never intrusive. She bent to pat the eager Jack Russell and smiled, "Take care both."

Within five minutes they were strolling along the mown path that led into the small wood on the outskirts of town, stopping every ten yards for a scent of something that just had to be investigated.

Her little companion was a rescue dog with an unhappy background, but she felt he had rescued her as much as the other way round. He had been with her for three years now and just as his confidence and trust had grown, so had hers.

These days she felt at peace.

The care her family had shown her during her dark days, continued with regular phone calls and visits. Her son was married now and she was Grandma to a three year old little boy and a two month old baby boy.

She loved the wood with its fresh, clear light, its calm, quiet coolness.

They walked companionably along the little paths stopping and investigating various plants or being still, listening to the bird song.

Coming eventually to her favourite tree, she settled down, her back against the trunk with the little dog settling beside her. The warm sun beamed down on them and where the gaps between the branches were wider the sun shone through, bathing them in glorious, uplifting light. She laughed gently, quietly, not wanting to disturb the peace, the tranquillity. Relaxing in this quiet and warmth, she fell asleep.

* * * * * * * * * *

She awoke with a shiver. What time was it? How long had she slept? The family would be arriving. She jumped up and immediately cried out. Her ankle had twisted under her and she was falling...falling forwards and fast. She put out her hands but too late, she fell heavily hitting her head against a large rock. Everything went dark.

* * * * * * * * * *

She began to stir as the sounds of whimpering came softly through the pain and darkness, then louder and a wet tongue on her cheek. A puzzled, concerned little face was watching her. A slow hesitant wag of tail accompanied her attempt to move. She felt nauseous, dizzy, shaking with cold and shock, how on earth was she to get home? Who knew where she was? Of course, Mrs Trelawney knew, would she remember and let her family know she had headed for the woods. She tried again to stand but the pain was excruciating. Thank goodness for her loyal companion who had come and snuggled anxiously beside her, providing some warmth from his little body.

* * * * * * * * * *

Suddenly she heard the crunch of footsteps on the woodland path, quickly followed by yelling, "Mum! Mum! Where are you?"

She cried out "I'm here, over here!"

A loud excited barking joined her cries and in no time at all her son and daughter appeared with relief evident on their faces. Together they gently helped her up and supporting her on both sides made their slow and careful way out of the wood.

Mrs Trelawney was waiting at the end of the path and was visibly relieved to see the trio emerge. "My dear. So thankful you and your little dog are safe." She smiled her thanks. They continued on to the fisherman's cottage...home...and as they drew nearer she could see the warm welcoming blaze of light streaming out of the open front door, where her daughter in law stood with young son at her side and cradling that beautiful new life, that baby boy.

With her daughter on one side and her son on the other and that hairy excitable bundle at her feet, she forgot the pain and knew only that she was safe with the people who really cared.

7   Some days he sat for hours – Maggie Bannister

In the small room, surrounded by the tools of his trade. Books, papers, unopened brown envelopes strewn on the floor, letters half-written, discarded at random. Poems screwed up and thrown in anger that would never be read. Some of the words might survive, sat on the desk, staring back at him, accusingly. He would stare back at them, wondering where they had come from. Sometimes a turn of phrase took his attention, pleased him, and he smiled with self-satisfaction.

Immediately the guilt returned then, at first creeping through his skin and then washing him through, flooding his senses, and the cold awareness of his reality struck like a cold hammer in his skull, taking his breath away. The memories were there again, twisting and writhing until he could bear it no longer. He reached for the bottle hidden behind the desk, took a swig, picking up the pen then and wrote as if his life depended on it.

8   How to Rob a Candy Store in Three Easy Steps –
Anila Syed

Fingers and Jonny are concerned when a new candy store opens in their town. Is Mrs. Fletcher really a sweet old lady or a crime boss?

Look, we knew the store was a front, but for what? We scratched our heads every time we thought about it, not knowing that the answer was stranger and weirder than anyone could imagine.

My name's Mickey – just call me "Fingers" – McGee. The cops call me a small-time crook, my Ma calls me Michael.

On the day the Candy Store opened, they gave out free Whizz Poppers to everyone who went in.

I went in with Jonny. No-one knows Jonny's real name. His nickname? We don't know how he got that. Everyone loves candy, Jonny more than most. He only has two front teeth left in his mouth. He calls the left one Franky, no-one knows what he calls the right one. Jonny's gerbil, Mitch goes almost everywhere with him. That's all you need to know about Jonny.

I hung back a little, dazzled by the bright colours of the candy that filled every shelf, but Jonny's no shrinking Parma Violet. He marched right up to the Manager, a shrivelled old lady with 'Edna' on her name badge and demanded to know what kind of joint she was running.

Edna smiled a gap-toothed smile and said, "What'll it be, Sonny? Gobstoppers?" She emphasized the 'gob' in gobstoppers. Her two front teeth were missing so she whistled!

Jonny was taken aback but pulled himself up just in time. "Listen, Lady. We run the racket round here, see?"

He was going to say plenty more, but a big gorilla poked his head around the plastic curtain in back. "That ain't no lady," he said. "That's Mrs. Fletcher."

Mrs. Fletcher? I knew my eyes were wide and Jonny looked like he had been slipped a Lemon Sour. We had only stumbled into the den of one of the meanest, nastiest, most legendary Crime Lords in the County. But what was her game? It could be anything from laundering, tax evasion to feeding too much sugar to little kiddies.

Over the next few weeks, we kept a wary eye on the shop – the local gangs, the cops, the Mas and Pas in the area. What was the scam? Apart from the most beautifully delicate confectionary we'd ever seen, nothing seemed to be going on. The shop was more popular than ever.

I was pulled in just for questioning about the Candy Store. I swore on my life, I had no idea.

I went to see Jonny to ask if he had heard anything. Jonny looked shifty, but I would have worried if he hadn't. His eye-contact told me something was wrong. Jonny almost never made eye-contact. A shiner blazed out of his face

"Jonny! What happened?" I asked.

He smirked sheepishly. I gasped. "Jonny! What happened to Franky?"

It was a direct message from Mrs. Fletcher to stay away. "I just went round the back to have a look," he said. "They have a humongous safe in there, Fingers." One of his eyes gleamed blackly. I could see exactly what he was thinking.

"We can't steal a safe, Jonny," I said. "Not from right under her nose?"

"We have to, Fingers," he said, earnestly stroking Mitch. "We have to show them who the real bosses are around here."

For months Jonny trained Mitch to climb through a window and press his little paws against a full-sized button. He pushed that little rodent nearly to the limit of his little gerbil endurance, making him practise over and over again.

"The trick, Fingers, will be to keep Mitch from being distracted by the candy," he explained. So for the next few weeks, poor little Mitch was put on a strict diet: chocolate, penny toffee chews, sweet popcorn, gummy sweets – every type of candy you could imagine. Finally, finally! Mitch was refusing to eat any more sweets. Even a picture of a sweet wrapper was sending him retching in the opposite direction.

One day Jonny called me over. "He's ready," he said. We steeled ourselves.

That night, Mitch was let into the letterbox in the front door of the Candy Store. An agonising seven minutes later, the fire alarm blared madly from somewhere inside.

"This is it!" Jonny whispered. We donned our balaclavas and broke into the back just as they were all escaping. I ran in and threw a burning rag into the shop so that, quickly enough, smoke filled the space to keep everyone out front.

My fingers rapidly went to work on the combination of the safe. I was pulling the heavy steel door open in six seconds and in another two minutes we were out and away, Mitch stowed in Jonny's pocket, the safe contents secure in my backpack.

The top few pages were recipes – Grandma's Honeycomb, Luxury Cheesecake, Chocolate Fondant – hundreds of desserts and sweets. Then began the 'Thank you's. First, we thought it was just a few thank you cards. But it was cards, letters, notes. There were cards from all over the country! From crime bosses and their families.

Mrs. Fletcher was supplying party treats and cakes for birthday parties and celebrations for nearly all the crime families – and they loved it. Jonny and I stared at the final item in the safe: It was a little black book that contained the names and delivery addresses of the Corliones, the Gambinos, the Lucianos, you name it. We nearly dropped that thing as if they were watching us through it.

"We've got them!" Jonny said. "They'll never know who took this and we can blackmail them with it for ever more."

I whooped quietly, my heart making more noise than my face! The Fletchers would be history. How would they ever suspect us?

In Jonny's pocket, Mitch licked icing sugar off his paws. Despite his training, despite his aversion therapy, no-one guessed that Turkish Delight would be his undoing. And all over the Candy Shop, little gerbil icing sugar footprints were waiting to be discovered as soon as the fire alarm was inactivated.

9   Counting in 7s – Maggie Bannister

She had always felt different. Shut out. Kept
out. Pushed out. Left out. As if she wanted to
join in anyway! Her choice, then, to stay on the
edge. To listen to the others. To try to
understand but soon reject the silliness, the
shallowness, the 'in' jokes which were apparently
essential to being part of the crowd.

At school there had been the Popular Girls
with their whispers, makeup, spray tans and false
eyelashes and their pretend tattoos only there
fleetingly to catch attention but not long enough
to spoil the perfection which took hours to attain
every morning. They weren't real. Only puffs of
smoke.

And the Naughty Girls, who seemed so
unhappy, vying for attention by being a nuisance,
being rude, hurting people. What was the point
of that?

Whereas she – she had a different path if only
she could find it, clouded by others' falsities and
pretence. Was this life? Pretending?

The adults at school had been just as bad.
Pretending to like her, pretending to be interested
in her work and then telling her to have more
'imagination', to write stories about people she
had never met, or draw pictures of things she had
never seen. Once she was told to copy a painting
for homework, so she did just that, meticulously
measuring and replicating the picture until her
parents told her that after 3 hours she had done
enough, even though she hadn't finished. The
next day the Art mistress explained that when

she had said 'copy' she hadn't meant 'copy' and she had laughed at her, as if telling lies was funny, when it really wasn't.

So instead, she counted. Enumerating the world into shapes and measurements and solid things that did not pretend to be something else. Numbers were her friends and became her entry into this strange world that everyone else, it seemed, was happy with. Numbers had colours and feelings, she discovered. 7 was a happy number, yellow and bright and pleasing to the senses. She liked to count music in 7s when she heard it, which wasn't very often. 9 was her comforting number: clever, solid and blue and it never got lost. Yes, numbers were her friends, here outside the world of noise and chaos, and on into infinity.

No-one seemed to understand her and nor did she, not yet. She lived in a world unattuned to her beauty, her melody, her ability to see into the smallest detail. Her eyes saw it all, were attacked by the light. which made her squint and cower from the brightness. Everyone else lived in a different dimension. They rushed in and blundered out and didn't NOTICE THE WORLD. She wanted to make them stop, but they wouldn't listen, couldn't see, shouldn't be allowed. With great precision she began to plan her revenge. She would destroy them, eliminate them, until all that remained were others like her, which she would manufacture herself. A perfect, controllable world.

10 On The Heath – Peter West

What is The Heath? Where is it, and why is it important?

It is any piece of undeveloped land where things grow wild and free. Most are natural, completely undeveloped areas; however, even once abandoned industrial sites can return to being "heathland." In this day and age, it might be a Nature Reserve or a place of natural beauty, often wooded but frequently just open moorland.

To many, it is a wild, unmanaged, seemingly abandoned area beyond where people usually venture, having an "unworldly" air, where strange, unaccountable things can happen. I think this explains why open spaces are often regarded with some suspicion.

Although nothing untoward is ever likely to occur without the hand of man being involved at some point!

Picture a dark, largely moonless night, a coach and four, or maybe five or six, horses, crossing the heath. The Coach has lights, enough to mark its presence to others and no more, sufficient to be taken down and used to light the way to the door once the destination is reached.

Such was travel in these times. In fact, journeys of any length at night are only for the foolhardy or the most urgent reasons...and perhaps the gallants and the audacious.

Think of what might happen – Perhaps a local man, hard-pressed to feed his family, is out "poaching" for the pot, or a Road-man or

Highway-man "on the rob", but something goes horribly wrong.

Did they, by chance, come across the wrong person, were they recognised, what to do? Life or death, decision time. Death by Hanging for Murder or Transportation for Robbery. Almost as bad, as few survived! Were they challenged with a pistol or sword? Split-second reaction, life, quite literally, on the edge!

The deed is done; somebody lost, but what to do now?

Blackened Bodies on the Heath!

11 Blood from a stone – Chris Westwood Marshall

In this case, (A) is working towards being a 'newly qualified teacher' i.e. in the first year of teaching and has been asked to support a more senior colleague in their classroom.

The teacher in training has been directed to assist a 15 year old girl (B) to write for the 'speaking and listening' portion of the English examination. The not yet NQT (A) knows it is their job but has no real idea or experience in how to get through entrenched apathy! Is this entrenched apathy?

Whatever it is, it's wrong innit?

A. So what do you want to talk about?

B. Abortion

A. OK. That's an interesting topic. What would you say about abortion?

B. It's wrong innit?

A. What's wrong about it?

B. It's just wrong innit?

A. What if the pregnancy was because of rape?

B. (Quiet and nonplussed for about a minute). Well that's wrong innit?

A. Yes but what's wrong about it? Can you think of any reasons why someone might feel they should have an abortion?

B. Well for rape.

A. Yes, but if you didn't want the child?

B. It's wrong innit?

A. Was there a particular reason you wanted to talk about abortion?

B. Yeah, it's wrong innit?

A. Would it be better to choose another topic where you had more to say?

B. I want to talk about abortion.

A. OK. What can you say about abortion?

B. (Silence)

A. Why is it wrong?

B. (Shaking head exasperatedly). It's wrong innit?

A. Well you can't just say it's wrong. This is supposed to be a 10 minute talk of your choosing followed by a discussion. I'm not sure you have enough to say. Would you like to choose another topic?

B. No

At this point the training NQT tries to disengage (if that constituted engagement at all!) but is unable to leave the situation unscathed (insides in turmoil) with 15 minutes left of the lesson!

12 So many colours – Maggie Bannister

The more I look the more I can see so I resist the temptation to use pencil. Not yet.

Mottled curves and not a straight line in sight.

It could be an animal skin, with its brown spots forming intricate patterns on the sunshine-coloured curves.

Or it could be a new moon on a slightly cloudy night.

Sweeping curves of yellow, bruised in places, hiding the sweet flesh.

I marvel at the distance it has travelled, wonder who picked it.

Truly a miracle that it is here at all.

Watercolours I think, quickly, before it ripens almost in front of my eyes.

13 Unfortunate George – Peter West

Always unfortunate, his father left when he was young, and his upbringing was a real struggle for his mother. His sister, several years older, seemed to do a bit better, as with her many boyfriends, she always had a little money to spend.

George didn't see much point in school, much too much bother when there were always things to do. Things like turning a penny here or a little earning job there, there was always something. You understand it was not always "regular"; that just wasn't his way, but it kept him in pocket money.

He met others just like himself; some he thought were clever, and others he despised, but, as people often said, it took all sorts!

There was always a new trick to pull, and often it took a little money to set things up, and this was where he "fell into a hole." His last job had failed, and he had borrowed money to set that one up. So, he put the word out, 'just had to try again.

And then, a stroke of fortune. A friend of a friend needed a hand, simple stuff, little involvement. "If you're interested and want to know more... it'll pay off what you owe...you know where to meet!"

George didn't like going there, not the nicest of places, the towpath under the bridge beside the canal, but he needed to keep things moving forward.

So, there he was at 11.30 at night, out on a limb to try to turn things around. After several minutes, it seemed more, a figure he thought he recognised stepped out of a shadow, then two more. Something's wrong here!

The three had come to teach those that borrowed from them a lesson. Iron bars and a heavy cosh laid into George, two broken legs, a dislocated shoulder and a severe concussion...and he was in the water!

Canals don't, as a rule, flow very much at all...but "our" George was lucky, oh lucky George? Just enough flow from the Sewage works, it had been raining quite hard earlier, to sweep him out into the Thames. It wasn't good along the way, being half-drowned and unable to do much about his predicament. When he happened to come to the surface, it was all he could do to breathe a little.

Things were getting grim, the water was colder, and he was drifting in and out of consciousness. Was there another sound besides the "slap" of water, a different, irregular "slap," and the sound of a motor?

Then a jarring blow to his body, searing pain...and the tiny, tiniest glimpse of blue light. Followed, thankfully, by the feeling of a solid, but moving, surface, and, eventually, a blanket was thrown over him.

14 Trouble in Town – Janet Cupit

She loved this part of town, the oldest street and still untouched. Most of the buildings were well over one hundred and fifty years old and the two pubs dating from the 1500's, with their carriage wide archways still very much intact, reminded her of a very different life, difficult to comprehend in today's modern, gadget and technology filled world.

Wandering down the narrow street, she paused often to gaze in the windows of these shops, owned by individuals not some huge, faceless, conglomerate. She tried to support them by buying what she could afford, even if it was only a card or a bag if sweets, a little jug for her collection.

She hated the modern shopping centre, pristine, shiny with no character, but there were a couple of ecofriendly shops that she liked to support and so she would venture in. Normally on a Saturday afternoon nothing fazed her; not the huge raucous groups of youngsters gathered in the shopping centre, discussing Friday night conquests nor the reeling drunks full of cheap booze. She strode confidently, almost aggressively through them all.

But today as she neared the end of the narrow street as it broadened out into the marketplace and on towards the glitzy centre, it felt different. There was an air, a tangible feel like just before a thunderstorm, an exciting yet oppressive and fearsome atmosphere.

Perhaps the seeds for this disquiet had been sown last week, seeing that tall muscular youth mocking a small silver haired woman, nothing violent, unpleasant that's all. She had cried out, "Leave her alone you big bully." At which the youth turned with a glaring look of hatred on his face and took a step towards her. She had retreated into a nearby shop, shaken and scared. When she looked through the window, she saw a crowd had gathered, the youth was beating a hasty retreat and someone had approached the old lady and with a comforting arm around her shoulders, led her away, presumably to buy her a cup of coffee.

She was so angry with herself, what a coward, retreating and hiding, what was wrong with her.....she felt ashamed.

Continuing across the marketplace she shrugged, how silly to think something was wrong on this beautiful sunny day. This was a good town to live in, what happened last week was rare, thank goodness.

She made her way through the crowded centre to the two eco shops and made her purchases, anxious to be out and on her way home.

Walking back up her favourite street she took time to admire the old buildings. All higgledy-piggledy, different bricks or stones, a fascinating variety of chimney pots, wonky windows....no set building regulations when these homes were built.

As she reached the first pub and its carriage wide entrance, a movement caught her eye. No

....it just couldn't be! It was the same burly youth from last week, this time with a mate and this time with an old man in their sights. She could hear them mocking him as he stood unsure what to do. Suddenly, the mate kicked out and the old man's walking stick clattered to the ground, closely followed by the old man who'd lost his balance. There was raucous laughter and then a cold voice said, "Money Grandad! And we might just leave you alone ...if you're lucky." She felt sick to her stomach. She wanted to run and find someone more capable to come and help.

No! not this time!

Reaching into her bag, she found her perfume spray. and secreted it into the palm of her hand. Putting down her shopping, she held onto her handbag by its long strap. She stepped into the covered way .

"Stop that now, you pathetic cowards" she cried...amazed that there was no quiver in her voice, no hesitancy. She sounded loud and strong. The bully turned and sneered, "What you gonna do about it b****?"

"This!!" she shouted and aimed her perfume spray at the two of them and while they took a shocked step back, she began to spin round.

Her handbag was at the full extent of the strap and as she turned the momentum increased. She could feel the bag coming into sharp contact with knees, shins, shoulders, hips. She knew she couldn't win on her own, but she was incandescent with rage.

Dizzy and exhausted, she stopped. By now a sizeable crowd had surrounded the four of them, drawn by the yells af anger and pain from the two youths. To her immense relief she saw two policemen break through the crowd, approach and handcuff the two dazed assailants who were still trying to work out what had happened. She reached down and helped the old man to his feet, retrieved his stick and made sure he was steady.

"Thank you my dear" he said in a wavering voice.

"Are you okay?" she asked.

He nodded.

Just then a man pushed through the crowds. "Dad are you okay? What's happened?" He spoke quietly to the old man, checking he was not hurt. Placing a reassuring hand on his dad's arm, he turned to thank his saviour, but she was nowhere to be seen.

Having retrieved her shopping, she made her way to the top of the street where it joined a busy main road. She was soon swamped by the people bustling back and forth, intent only on their own problems and completely unaware of the drama that had taken place only yards away.

She smiled. There you are, she thought, you can be strong and stick up for what is right. I'm proud of you.

She didn't need the accolades and effusive thanks of others. The old man was safe. She had proved to herself that she could be strong when

needed and could stand up against the world's
bullies and for her, that was enough.

History and Politics

15 On the Radio – Chris Westwood Marshall

At some time during my day, I listen to the dulcet tones of reporters and presenters on Radio 4. In my car I listen, in my kitchen I listen, on my laptop I listen. I do enjoy listening and allowing the conjured images to ignite memory or cause me to debate internally on an issue that is new to me, or I become aware of a new angle that I had not considered before.

Today I was enjoying a brief talk about hands – an old song was played that I recognised, and I felt sad when I remembered the hands of my mother. She had beautiful long fingers, piano players delight but what I will never forget is that I cannot remember her hands being anything else but scratchy and coarse like sandpaper. She had eczema all the time I knew her and her hands despite creams and lotions from the doctor were made up of broken skin and half healed scratches. It was only her hands that had eczema but I was reluctant to hold her hands when I was small – that makes me sad for her and for me.

What brought me up short today was the mention of the hands of an orang-utan. A beautiful memory surged into my being followed by an angry image and angry words that tried to annihilate that recollection with what I can only believe to be arrogance and stupidity – nothing to do with the religion that was purported to be offended. I feel kinship to all my brethren and so I should.

I have learned in the last 2 weeks that I have a higher-than-average remnant of Neanderthal DNA in my gene pool. I'm 99 point something percent British, Irish and Western European – 8% of that is Scandinavian which I already suspected but the Neanderthal was interesting. I have Oddbod from 'Carry On Screaming' sitting in my mind's eye along with Dithers the gardener in a comedy with Ronnie Barker – the joke was his mass of hair and total incompetence. Neanderthal is the poster of the ape turning human with each step and my ancestors were in the middle of that poster somewhere. I have my second toe taller than my big toe which is a Neanderthal feature I shared with my mother. I knew but to have it confirmed is awesome.

With my new-found knowledge I have revisited the beautiful memory and the spoiling of it and want to do an 'I was right' dance because I was and I am.

I was in Tenerife Zoo in the heat in the late 1980s or early1990s. The trip was last-minute but we went to the zoo twice, the second time to take food. The keepers were nothing like those at London Zoo and we could get near the animals. That's when I held the hand of a mother orang-utan – held her hand through the bars of her cage. Her baby was equivalent to a ten-year-old human I think as it was with her but not dependant on her. It looked curiously at me as I held on to its mother's hand. I looked at the fingers of the fully grown ape, long like my mothers and soft with extra padding on the underside. Intelligence and beauty lived with that creature and I knew that I was part of her family.

No revulsion at the thought, why would there be revulsion associating the beautiful auburn-haired creature with my kith and kin. Neanderthal's R Us. Apes are us wearing slightly different suits. I'm more ape-like than the average – cool.

My memory was tarnished in the mid 1990s.

* * * * * * * * * *

I am an English teacher in my classroom. East London secondary school. We have a mixture of ethnicity in the room – I am a mixture of ethnicity with a tiny bit of Anatolian which of course I was unaware of at this time. I'm talking to the class. A topic is brought up – no idea what prompted it but the reaction stuns me. I have glazed over talking in wistful contemplation about those intelligent, soulful eyes and those hands so like mine. I'm back in Tenerife Zoo in my head and I can picture the hand hold that lasted for more than minutes. Darwin's general point, even if there are errors, has always made total sense to me. I point out that human hands and ape hands are too similar to not have some form of kinship. Stunned silence. I am an experienced teacher but I have never come across that fear – fear of being seen as stupid like an ape is clearly part of it for some of the kids – the fear of the Neanderthal knuckle scraping image of the East End.

One boy, though, is adamant and oozes disgust at the certainty I hold. He challenges me, dripping venom. He uses his faith as a shield, some nonsense about human beings' superiority and god-given right and total dissociation from the idea of kinship with any other being on the planet. I wonder if he tortures cats in his spare time. The kids are of different faiths and none but they collude with his dismissal. A mutiny of voices taints that memory of the majesty of ape and human holding hands.

Today I reclaim and reassert my kinship to those intelligent and hairy Neanderthal and Orang-Utan Apes and to the humans who besmirch their memory I wish them Mother Earth's forgiveness for they know not what they do.

16 Revelation – Robert Greener

Chapter 1 of "Journey to Dreamland"

July 1734, Canton Zürich

On a day that was mostly like any other, the world suddenly grew for Johann Ulrich, "Hans," and his young family. He did not feel young; he was in the 35th year of his life, which had begun just before the dawn of the eighteenth century. It had been a long, hot July day in the tailor shop where he laboured as a journeyman for the benefit of Lorentz, the Master. Rivulets of sweat ran down his face as he stretched away the cramps in his back and thighs, the product of hours sitting cross-legged on the table before the window, cutting and sewing the coats and dresses of the wealthier citizens of the little town in the Canton of Zürich. The working day was finally over – or at least the part of it for which he was paid. Tending the meagre crop on his small patch of land still awaited.

Hans set out for the 30-minute walk to his village home, his shoulders hunched. Always there was so much work to do, and so little in return. He prayed daily for some kind of delivery from the endless drudgery, but so far the Good Lord had answered with silence. Last winter had been a hard one, there was barely enough to eat. His two youngest children, one only six-months old, had contracted some kind of fever and died within days of one another. His wife, Verena, was inconsolable and was only recently emerging from the grief. Hans felt helpless to do anything about it, she had grown so distant from him.

If he thought too hard about it, Hans also worried about his prospects. There was little chance of advancement in the tailor's shop – he had got as far as being allowed to sew buttonholes, but any skilled position above that was already taken by men of his own age. Then there was talk among his fellow workers of yet another war brewing to the north, great powers beyond the Canton, quarrelling over succession to a throne far away that no-one knew anything about. These matters seemed beyond his understanding – the only thing Hans knew about it was that it would bring nothing good to his struggling family.

As he trudged along enmeshed in his dark thoughts, he was hailed by a familiar voice belonging to his friend Heinrich, who had an excited look in his eye and was waving what looked like a sheaf of paper. He slowed his stride to allow Heinrich to catch up, whereupon he thrust the paper at Hans.

"Have you seen this? It looks like paradise!"

Hans stared at the printed script of the newspaper. While he had learned some of his letters, these ones looked a bit too spidery and formal for him. He could however see that it was a newspaper printed a few days earlier in the nearby city of Zürich. He thrust it back at Heinrich, shaking his head.

"What does it say?"

Heinrich looked apologetic and smiled. "So many things! There's a place called Carolina Island, where Swiss people are living. It says the place is blissful! It looks like they are asking people to apply – there is a booklet for sale that tells all about it!"

Hans thought for a few moments, he had heard customers talking to the Master about a place they called 'Carolina Island.' It seemed to Hans that the place was a long way away, but one customer had talked about receiving a letter from a cousin who was living there somewhere.

All the same this newspaper article sounded fantastical, too good to be real, but a small light went on in a corner of his mind. What if this were true? Was this the sign that he had been waiting for? There were questions...

"How far away is Carolina Island?"

"It doesn't say, but it must be across the sea if it's an island."

"Can we find out more? How do we apply?"

"I don't know, but like I said there's a booklet that explains everything. But it costs three schillings...," he looked crestfallen, "Maybe someone will have a copy that we can see..."

Hans was thinking. This was a big, important newspaper from the city after all, the story must therefore be at least somewhat true. The whole thing sounded pretty good to him and the light in his mind was growing brighter, driving away some of the darkness.

But not all of it, there were too many
questions. Would the City authorities allow
anyone to go – they had rules about that? He
also didn't feel that he could spare three
schillings for a booklet – that was more than a
day's wages. An idea came to him.

"We should ask everyone at church. Maybe
someone knows more..."

Heinrich nodded as he peeled away towards
his home. "See you on Sunday."

* * * * * * * * * *

Verena looked up from her needlework when she
heard the arrival of her husband. She had been
attending to some clothing repairs for the
children, her task despite her husband's trade,
while also trying to keep them out of mischief.
Her eldest daughter, also called Verena, aged 9,
insisted on trying to help, although her sewing
skills were not adequate to the task, and what
she had managed would only have to be re-done.
She had sent the girl out of the room to find her
two younger brothers, Felix and Hans, who she
suspected were tormenting their youngest sister
Margaretha. By the sound of it, they had all been
playing some kind of hiding game, hopefully
without breaking anything. The two boys had
spotted their father and abandoned their game to
run out and greet him.

Verena could immediately see that he had
something on his mind, he had that faraway look
in his eyes, as if he had discovered something
new. She felt they had become strangers since
losing the two little ones, there was a tension

between them that lingered even after the months that had passed since the two tiny coffins were lowered into the cold ground. Hans had probably done his best to help, but had not spoken of them since, and she couldn't understand his apparent indifference. The family had shrunk from six children to four – Verena, Felix, little Hans Ulrich and three-year old Margaretha, but still she fretted about finding food for them all. There was so much in this world that could strike you down when you least expected it. What more could lie in store for the defenceless?

Verena was about to find out.

When Hans walked in, with two young boys clinging to his legs, Verena set aside her mending and got up to begin the meal preparation. She expected him to give up his news in due course, once the children were out of the way, but Hans could not contain himself.

"I walked home with Heinrich. He showed me something."

Verena silently waited for more.

"There is a new place we can go, where everything is better than here."

Verena sighed, "What kind of place?"

"It's called Carolina Island. Lots of Swiss people have gone there."

Verena had never heard of Carolina Island, and she didn't know any Swiss people who had gone there. She didn't think Hans did either.

"Where did Heinrich see this?" Verena didn't like Heinrich much, there was something about the way he looked at her.

"It's in the newspaper. The Donnstags-Nachrichten"

Verena still didn't like the sound of it. "How big is this island? How many people can fit there?"

Hans was getting annoyed. "It must be big enough or they wouldn't ask for more people."

"But our home is here. We cannot afford..."

"In the name of God, woman, do you hear what I am saying? We can make everything better!"

Verena knew better than to question the name of the Almighty out loud when Hans was in this mood. She looked at her young children, hoping they were oblivious to the raised voices, but determined to protect them if Hans continued to pursue this unlikely idea. She nodded mutely and stood. "I need to start cooking."

Verena half expected that the whole thing would go away of its own accord, but she resolved to find out what she could from her own friends.

* * * * * * * * * *

Sunday rolled around and Hans led his family along the road to the village church, unadorned in the way of the reformed faith, but still by far the grandest building for miles around. Despite his earnest enquiries to his puzzled friends and acquaintances, there seemed to be no further information. Nobody at the church knew anything, although a few had seen the newspaper in question, and some were interested to know more.

Hans was frustrated and impatient, but had not lost his resolve. As luck would have it, he came upon Heinrich once again a week later, once again carrying a newspaper and looking excited.

"There's more, in here! Look!"

Hans had to shake his head again.

"More information about this booklet that describes Carolina! They call it the 'Holy Land' – the people there must be of the reformed faith, like us!"

This sounded even better to Hans – a place to worship God in the proper way.

But Heinrich hadn't finished. "It says the place is very fertile, and the air is clean! The Swiss people living there don't ever want to come back!"

Hans thought of his little patch of potatoes multiplied to a field of plenty. He pictured a growing family of healthy children living in safety and godliness. He pictured a life where he was his own master – no more endless stitching in the fading light. Perhaps even buying his own clothes made by someone else's hand. There had to be a way to get a copy of this booklet.

The church on Sunday was more lively with rumours, it seemed that their enquiries the previous week had lit a fire in more than one mind. These rumours became attached to news about an influential person, when the minister announced that there would be a guest preacher visiting the church on the following Sunday. This would be a man who would have interesting things to say to anyone who might be seeking a new life. The minister said no more, but the implication seemed obvious to the likes of Hans, obsessed with his vision of paradise.

The man in question did have quite some reputation. Even Hans had heard of him, in both positive and negative ways. He spent the week in a ferment of curiosity and hope, to the despair of his long-suffering wife whose enthusiasm clearly did not match his own. The following Sunday arrived in an atmosphere of expectation.

Mauritz Götschi was known as a firebrand preacher with hints of immoral behaviour that had seen him dismissed from the ministry. It was widely known that the behaviour in question had resulted in at least one illegitimate child and resulted in a custodial sentence. There was some uncertainty about whether he was still allowed to preach at all, certainly not in the City. And yet here he was, ebullient and unapologetic, and clearly on good terms with the local minister, who stood by nodding his head.

Despite some muttering, the congregation heard him out, and were treated to a tour de force. He had not simply seen the newspaper articles that had so intrigued Hans, he had obtained a copy of the booklet, which he waved about as his voice thundered out through the chamber.

He began in the usual fashion for a full-blooded sermon, remonstrating against ungodly thoughts, which Hans thought he must know quite something about. That dispensed with, the man's booming discourse turned to matters of state, railing against the doomed fate of the ungodly in the unreformed Cantons, and the threat posed by the warring Catholic empire to their north, too close for comfort. To Hans, his words confirmed all of his fears, he could feel the power of truth. Hans began to doubt that there was truth in the accusations against Götschi, the man spoke with conviction as if voiced by one who had found favour with almighty God himself.

To the astonishment of Hans and most of the congregation, Götschi pointed to the booklet in his hand. He repeated the words of the newspaper articles that had stirred Hans's heart, and proclaimed them as heralding the building of a new world, nothing less than a summoning of the faithful to a paradise of their own making. He announced that he was making an application to the town council of Zürich to lead an expedition to Carolina Island to found a new church and community of Swiss folk. He was visiting all of the villages in the Canton, compiling a list of interested parties.

Hans was an interested party.

It was clear from the distressed expression on her face that his wife was not. He decided he would deal with that problem later and went forward to add his name.

He was not the only one in the line.

17 Is that it? – Chris Westwood Marshall

LEGAL BOD:
>   So, let me get this straight, you're telling
>   me he had his hands round your throat
>   and you didn't leave?

FEMALE (GENERALLY):
>   Well, when you put it like that you make
>   me sound like a complete moron,
>   someone who was asking to be treated
>   like that. It was the only time he actually
>   touched me – punching the walls was
>   more his thing. Do you leave if someone
>   punches a wall? I don't know.
>
>   My dad never punched walls but maybe
>   that was just my dad – maybe most guys
>   punch walls - it's not as if I've lived with
>   loads of men and know that they don't
>   have their hands round your throat or
>   punch walls. My mum didn't mention
>   anything about throats and walls –
>   maybe she should have.
>
>   So you're saying I've got no chance of
>   controlling his access to the kids? I just
>   want someone else around.

LEGAL BOD:
>   Evidence. Photographs. Proof. Where is
>   it? Are we just supposed to take the
>   word of someone who allows their
>   partner to put his hands round their
>   throat?

FEMALE:
>   When you put it like that – I sort of get it.
>   But are my kids safe with a man who

punches walls and has his hands around his partner's throat? He did say it was because the washing machine was too loud by the way – is that a good reason? Said I'd turned it on deliberately to annoy him.

My dad never had his hands round my mum's throat over the washing machine. My dad bought my mum an electric one in 1969 and the whole family sat and watched the first whole wash cycle from beginning to end. There were tears in my mum's eyes – she was so happy to see that twin tub get carted away.

Come to think of it the offending machine was a twin tub – I was the only worker in the household at the time and I'd been offered it cheap. I bought an electric washing machine, one from Zanussi that said it was extra quiet. I got it as soon as I realised that the twin tub could have got me killed. I don't think it's fair to kill someone over a twin tub – my dad was very reasonable, I suppose, looking back.

LEGAL BOD:

Well, your mum and dad were married. That makes the difference. Your mum could've taken your dad to the cleaners (pardon the pun) if he had tried to strangle her. That's what you get for not being married – no security.

FEMALE:

Yes. How stupid of me. A piece of paper always protects you from people intent

on harming you. It makes complete
sense to me now. How silly of me. It was
all my fault.

LEGAL BODS:

And he isn't named on the birth
certificates. Your children are bastards
then?

FEMALE:

When you put it like that, I sound like a
complete slag don't I? The image of the
woman with loads of different baby
daddies, living in squalor and scrounging
off the state. But it wasn't like that and
for the record I don't think the stereotype
is fair anyway – so much crap to wade
through I'd be here all night. He waited
until my eldest was in the world before
he said he didn't want to have his name
on the birth certificate. I was a
secondary school teacher. It was the
1990s (supposed to be progressive and
all that).

I thought he'd be on the birth certificate
though – hadn't questioned that idea for
a second. I think he did it to shock and
demoralise – he liked to see the outrage
on my mum's face – suppressed stiff
upper lip outrage is possibly funny to
someone who likes to torture, someone
who likes to put hands round people's
throat and squeeze. Is that a fit father to
give your children to? One who isn't
even named on the birth certificate.

LEGAL BOD:

> He has to appeal to the courts and get parental responsibility. You've told me nothing that won't get him that right. We all have our foibles. I'm sure he had his reasons.

FEMALE:

> Yes, at the time if you weren't named on the birth certificate you didn't have to pay for your kids – perfect deniability. DNA wasn't really a thing then for ordinary people. He told me it was because he had some Jewish ancestry. Didn't want his kids targeted in another holocaust. Sounded plausible but now he's demanding that his name is on their birth certificates so he and his new wife can play happy families.

LEGAL BOD:

> You sound bitter.

FEMALE:

> She's really welcome to him. She can have him and his throat hands and his pedantry and his love of torture and his hatred of twin tubs. It's not bitterness. It's that it seems like he's going to get away with not wanting to be their dad when it suits him and because he's married that makes him plausible and decent – he's playing the system and you're letting him. Marriage is his get out of jail free card as much as not being married was his get out of jail free card. It simply isn't fair.

LEGAL BOD:

You should have been married. You could have taken him to the cleaners.

FEMALE:

Yes of course, how silly of me. Next time I have children with someone who's told me that although they've had their hands round my throat it doesn't mean they don't care about me. Like I'm going to fall for that one again. Besides I'm in my forties – any female over forty is lucky to get a second glance on these new apps.

LEGAL BOD:

Well, whatever you do don't warn your children that he likes to punch walls or have his hands round your throat. That will be considered parental alienation. The courts take a dim view of mothers who bad mouth fathers.

FEMALE:

But he's not on the birth certificate. The kids are mine in law. My dad even pointed that out to me. You're taking away my right to not have him on the birth certificate. I don't want a guy who hates twin tubs on my children's birth certificates – intolerance towards twin tubs is not an attitude I want passed on to the kids. And he has a police record. From before I knew him. Aggressive verbal assault on an undercover policeman. Is that a safe dad for the kids? Can someone at least look into

that – someone with professional
training.

LEGAL BOD:

You seem to be making this up. You
keep adding objections – really don't say
anything to your kids.

FEMALE:

They've already seen the wall punching –
they could hardly miss it. My eldest
can't remember the scary shake at 2
weeks old but the youngest knows that
his wrist break was his dad's fault – he
was there.

LEGAL BOD:

Evidence? Proof?

FEMALE:

I've got the x-rays but no proof. I wasn't
there. But I believe the 6-year-old who
loves animals and Lego over the twin tub
hater.

LEGAL BOD:

Did you coach him?

FEMALE:

What?

LEGAL BOD:

Did you tell your son what to say?

FEMALE:

No. I don't go around making up stories.
It's not as if I regularly live with blokes
and have children who get their wrists
broken by those blokes. I don't have
Munchausen by proxy – make a

mountain out of a mole hill to get the
authorities to praise me for my amazing
mothering skills and my fortitude with
sick children. I don't slip my children
drugs or injuries as a way to get
attention. I get enough attention in my
classroom thank you.

LEGAL BOD:

And you say he's been sending you
threatening texts?

FEMALE:

Yeah. He keeps trying to get my address
when I don't want him there – I feel safe
knowing he can't just show up and then
he does just that. Sends me this text
saying he's outside my home and he's
sorry to have missed me. He's sent me
others too – one where he said I had no
right to not let him see the kids and he
was coming to take the eldest away with
him. As the only parent on the birth
certificate surely it is my right to say
what happens with the kids.

I have been taking the kids to our joint
home (the one he's refused to leave) every
other weekend for 3 years. I didn't want
him to know my address cos I didn't
fancy any throat thing or wall punching
or him acting as if nothing has happened
and asking me to put the kettle on and
rifling through my fridge for food. It'd be
like I'd never left.

I've lived with him for 20 years you see. I
know he'll try and get his way through

intimidation or feigned affability
whichever works in whatever order. It
has nothing to do with the kids, nothing
to do with love for the kids. If he loved
the kids he wouldn't punch walls in front
of them, threaten our daughter because
she talked over a TV show he liked, or be
responsible for breaking our son's wrist.
I should like to point out that at present
they are technically my kids – he's still
not on the birth certificates.

LEGAL BODS:

This seems like a very complex case –
we're going to have to charge you more.
If only you were married, the case would
be a lot simpler. You could have taken
him to the cleaners. Those text
messages are inadmissible in court by
the way, and I've seen far worse. There's
only a few here – real abusers send
hundreds.

FEMALE:

Oh how silly of me – to talk about abuse
when there's women out there being
beaten black and blue. I really think
that's bad but why don't you get that
there is more than one way to hurt
someone – don't give me that sticks and
stones crap. The problem is because
society doesn't recognise bad behaviour if
she isn't being beaten to a pulp, neither
do the people on the receiving end of the
bad behaviour. You just want abuse
porn to line your pockets, make it easy
for you in the courts. You want stories of

'real' brutality to titillate the media outlets, have everyone say 'gosh that's awful' and marvel at how she didn't manage to see it coming. She should have known. Open your fucking ears and listen.

LEGAL BOD:

You're very aggressive. You won't get anywhere with a temper like that. Calm down dear. Maybe we should give the kids to their father. Maybe they'd be safer. I'm sure his wife will be nice and sensible and respectable – after all, she's married.

18 On Aran Jumpers and Ponchos, Hot Pants and Kinky Boots – Chris Westwood Marshall

1974. A lounge with a television. Me, aged 12 sitting in that lounge alone watching 'rubbish' on the telly – my mother's words. An earlier version of me would have sat obliviously watching that box wearing my Aran Jumper or my red poncho, both knitted by my Grandma. Aged 12 I remember the old French guy, with the wavering voice singing 'She'. I thought his voice was an old man's voice but evidently he was meant to be seen as 'romantic' because of his 'emotional' voice and his foreign accent. He would have been on 'Top of the Pops ' and to me he would have been completely out of place, just like Pavarotti seemed to be 'out of place' to me two decades later.

I'd been brought up on assessing singers for their looks and 'old men' weren't on any radar that I possessed. Nana Mouskouri looked out of place to me too, so it wasn't just the men. Although Mary Hopkins had passed muster in the 1960s, probably because my appraisal button hadn't kicked in then. My generation were fed 'The Monkees', 'Slade', 'T-Rex', Rod Stewart, 'Roxy Music', 'Queen', 'David Bowie' '10cc'. I know the list is far longer and predominantly male. I was a little young for Beatlemania but I saw it on the news. What was a 12-year-old female supposed to make of all this 'entertainment' – songs sung by 'pretty boys' with their inconsistent messages about love and loss and heartbreak and the implicit views on femininity. Were we there to swoon and admire, look good, find a man, have babies and then be abandoned when someone more desirable came along?

It was a given that we would deserve to be abandoned if we weren't up for kinky boots, walking all over you. And what if you were never the face that couldn't be forgotten? How were you supposed to be an aggressive go-getting woman who knew what she wanted particularly in the bedroom. I never understood why Cat Stevens was 'looking for a hard-headed woman'

I was the same 'girl' who had been fed Ada Dawson and Cissy, Olive from 'On the Buses', Hill's 'scantily clad' Angels (all women), Pan's 'scantily clad' People (all women), Dick Emery's Hetty and Mandy to again name just a few. All 'women' were portrayed as either 'desperate for it', hideous to look at or sexually alluring and willing to show it. They were also unkind gossips and unforgiving critics. There was never such an array of ways of being among men because they were not dependant on reputation or appearance – they were never considered as having a shelf-life. Old men were still heart throbs if the old narratives were to be believed.

On that box in the corner we had 'The Liver Birds' struggling with the aspiration to be independent and the desire to be married with children – it was a given that all women wanted the latter even if they didn't voice it. My Aunt Jean had never been a 'Pontefract Bird' or married and two of my mum's three brothers were married with children and had wives who were clinging in there to the bitter end. Nothing I saw on the TV was playing in my lived experience but still it became a blueprint of sorts. Freud blamed our fathers for how we turned out – my dad was too busy getting through life and had little time to assess the impact of this television phenomena had on his children.

Schizophrenia is supposed to be disorganised thinking and holding beliefs that are not based in reality. What about the conflicting beliefs we were fed, the 'non sense'. Where is a 'female' supposed to stand? Our lives have never followed Hollywood scripts. We leave the planet incomplete just the same as we arrive, trailing those clouds of glory, that potential that can never be realised because we're no longer here to see the impact our lives have made.

'None at all' as the great Douglas Adams said.

Does a world fantasy exist? Does there need to be a world understanding that counteracts any fantasy? Particularly where females are concerned? The way things are rather than the way we want them to be which is influenced by a cultural consensus that defies common sense.

Kinky Boots tended to be black, high-heeled and made of leather – Emma Peel and Purdy and the Avengers come to mind. Whitehouse challenged the morality but no one pointed out the obvious – high heels put your back out. Hot Pants were only good in the summer but you did have to contend with both overt and furtive ogling and that old excuse 'she made me do it – she shouldn't have worn those clothes' sitting there unchallenged for decades. Instead Mrs Whitehouse and her ilk endlessly picked at the morality or lack of it – no decent girl would go out looking like that. What on earth is a decent girl? Why are Aran jumpers or red ponchos knitted by your Gran seen as the hallmark of decency?

'Cover up properly' were the words of an older generation. Surely what is 'proper' should have remained a conversation for the Victorians but it morphed in the 1920s and then again in the 1960s. A complete overhaul of the rules dominated the 1960s - the 'anything goes' approach which was far in excess of the 'glimpse of stocking' that the 1920s were challenging. Were Aran jumpers 'safety' like Ron Weasley's handmade sweaters? If you tried to stay safe in the world avoiding the trappings of kinky clothes you were considered to be behind the times. I remember the furore about hot pants being available in shops for 9-year-olds and younger in the 1970s. Were they designed to titillate? And why were we mocked for being uptight and prudish if we didn't take the kinky boot route?

At college in 1981 I was told to stop 'prick teasing', to stop 'holding out'. Apparently we all wanted it really. I understand that in 2023 college campuses and even schools are now fraught with unrealistic expectations and sexual assault.

Is there a commodity feel to that expectation on women? Are we supposed to be able to turn it on and off like a tap – that sexual desire and abandoned sexual activity. I believe it has lead to the current Incel problem where some guys believe women are 'putting it about' with 'anyone' except them – and our media induced fantasies don't help. My generation were still caught between two worlds although that was never acknowledged at the time and the lines still seem blurred. Sexual freedom surely means we have choice, there should be no expectation or compulsion but it is evident in the non-disclosure payouts made to victims of unwanted sexual advances, that we, as a society, have a problem. Are women still having to choose between Aran Jumpers and Kinky Boots? Religious morality is just another weapon in the wrong hands as is the instruction to 'let your hair down'. I believe there should be a real discussion on the definition of 'a woman's right to choose' and it needs to stop centring on our appearance or morality. It is a conversation that is long overdue.

19 Bugexit <u>means</u> Bugexit – Anila Syed

"Everything's such a mess!"

The Right Honourable Lenny Winger, Member of Parliament for Haverford West, gazed out moodily across the House of Commons' Debating Chamber. It was late, really late. Although his Hygiene Debate had seemed like such a great idea, the reality of it all was only just beginning to hit home.

His colleague, Reginald Wright was the only other person present. After two years of thrashing out the same arguments, no-one else even bothered to turn up anymore.

Reginald shrugged: "The people have spoken," was all he could say for the eighteenth time that day.

"Have they?" Lenny asked, irritated. "Have they?

"Did they really know, that when they wanted the germs gone, it would mean all the germs?"

Reginald shrugged again. A hopeless sort of despair had haunted his eyes for the best part of a week now. And whenever he had to parrot one of the 'mantras' (the people have spoken, Bugexit means Bugexit, three hundred and fifty million fewer microbes a second in the UK), a muscle in his left cheekbone, high up somewhere, twitched crazily, giving him the appearance of a lecherous buffoon, winking at everyone present.

"You'd better stop that lecherous twitching or the Fortune Teller will have you up in front of the Committee," Lenny said.

The two of them were friends, despite being normally seated on opposite sides of the House.

"I know," Reginald said, morosely. "She's only keeping me around because it will be useful to have someone to throw under a bus later on."

"Uh oh, look sharp, they're switching the cameras on," Lenny said.

Both men jumped into their seats, Lenny took his phone out and began texting in a bored way; Reginald stood to attention, one arm raised oratorically, while a humorous grin played about his ruggedly handsome jawline.

"…and so I say to you, Madam Deputy Speaker, the people have spoken! Bugexit means Bugexit. There will be three hundred and fifty million fewer microbes a second in the UK…"

* * * * * * * * * *

In the flat above her official residence, the Fortune Teller slumped onto the couch, slipped off her nude shoes and massaged one calf tenderly. She had been wearing the same shoes for nearly eighteen hours non-stop. After a certain point in time, the heels stopped providing support and started to dig up into the soles of her feet, indicating a certain lack of mercy, she supposed. An insincere thought about the members of her Cabinet fleetingly surfaced into her consciousness.

She shrugged mentally as she regarded the discarded husks of 'shoe' lying on the deep pile rug. When she had been a young intern all those years ago, these shoes would have been called a mushroom colour. Now they were called nude because mushroom was boring. But whatever they were called through the years, the fact remained that they were beige. If only people could see that, she thought. If only people could be made to see, no, forced to see that beige is beige, whatever fancy word you use to describe it.

She'd just spent eighteen hours on a press junket being driven up and down the country and she wasn't sure that the media understood her message any more clearly than they had yesterday. Why couldn't she just stand up in front of them all and say, 'Open your eyes, fools! It's beige! It's been beige all along!'

She covered her face soothingly with one hand. Did any of that make sense? It had been fine a second before she had thought it, but the moment the thought was in her brain it lost all meaning. Maybe that was the problem. She leaned back onto the couch and was asleep before her head touched the cushion.

* * * * * * * * * *

"Why is she called the Fortune Teller then?" Lenny asked Reginald in the House of Commons Tea Room.

"It's because she used to be one," came the answer.

"What? She was so insightful that she could make truthful predictions about the politics of the day?" Lenny said, taking up a scone and examining it closely.

"No, she used to be a fortune teller. An actual one, in a circus." Reginald quickly took up the last remaining scone, in case his friend had his eye on it.

"Apparently, she was so bad at it, that she jacked it all in and became a politician. She's never looked into a crystal ball again, apparently. Never needed to.

"We voted her in because the other guy was more of a bumbling idiot and he wanted Bugexit. Practically forced the referendum, I heard. Made up some kind of dossier about why there was a historical reason that the people should be allowed to decide whether we should let foreign bugs into the country. Apparently, there wasn't an ounce of science in it. Someone told me he pinched most of the ideas from a kid's school project." Reginald finally took a bite of the scone.

"A kid's sci-fi drama project," he said with his mouth full, pointing the rest of the scone at Lenny for emphasis.

"But why does she want to see us?" Lenny said. "It's making me nervous.

"You voted 'Clean' and I voted 'Stain.' We're at opposite ends."

"Had to," Reginald interrupted, still chewing. "My constituents wanted to get rid of the bugs."

"I know, old chap, I know," Lenny said, consolingly. "No-one told them the facts, that's why."

They both leaned back into their leather armchairs. The gloom in the room was tangible. It was funny how, since the Hygiene Referendum had shocked the country by deciding to get rid of all bugs, everything had seemed to be covered in more grime and uncertainty than ever before.

* * * * * * * * * *

"You wanted to see us, Fortune Teller?" Lenny said, after a couple of short coughs had been ignored.

The Fortune Teller was seated at her desk, head in her hands. She looked up, blearily coming into focus after a second. "Ah, yes," she said. "Sit down!"

* * * * * * * * * *

"...so what you mean to say is that despite the presence of things like salmonella, listeria, and even Pseudomonas aeruginosa, the vast majority of bacteria are actually good bacteria which help us to function, break down our food and may even have moved into our cells once, a long time ago to give us energy?" Reginald let out a long, slow whistle.

The past three and half hours had been enlightening to say the least. He would remember it for years to come as a montage of black and white stills:

The Fortune Teller looking conciliatory. Lenny Winger and Reginald Wright looking disbelieving, sceptical, at times, downright hostile. The Fortune Teller running them through a short PowerPoint about the benefits of the human microbiome that she had downloaded from a primary school website. The three of them gazing wondrously at each other as the penny finally dropped: Bugexit did not have to mean Bugexit.

Lenny clutched at his bald pate, a look of euphoria on his face. "In fact, it could mean disaster; a cataclysmic meltdown; the end of all things," he said, looking triumphantly at the other two. He clutched at his sides through his ill-fitting suit, but he was unable to contain the giggles. This could possibly really be the answer they had all been looking for. Unexpectedly, unwantedly, completely uncharacteristically, they planned to use the truth to win their political argument. What was the world coming to?

* * * * * * * * * *

"But why did she choose us?" Lenny asked Reginald for the eighteenth time.

"Dunno," Reginald said, absentmindedly. "She said that she saw us in the House of Commons – at that 3am debate we went to. She said that she recognised a sort of commitment that she could work with."

"Great."

* * * * * * * * * *

The Fortune Teller smoothed down the short, puffy jacket that her PR made her wear. Why they gave her such unflattering clothes she would never know. With her long legs and slightly hunched posture, the short jackets and long-line trousers made her look like a character from Monty Python. There was always a reason: The polls showed that the people did not want an attractive person in charge. In fact, the more unappealing the personage, the better chance they had to get voted in, apparently. If all else failed, an unattractive spouse would also serve the same purpose.

She glanced over at Nigel. Well, she had not been blessed with an unattractive spouse, so, short jackets it would have to be.

The people were never wrong.

She checked her smile in the hallway mirror and, with Reginald and Lenny at her side, opened the door of No. 10. A wall of flashbulbs assaulted her senses as she fought her way to the single microphone situated in front of The Press.

"Fortune Teller, can you tell us about your change of heart?"

"Fortune Teller, look this way!"

"Fortune Teller, can you tell us if there is any new information about Bugexit?"

She waited for the shouting to die down before speaking:

"For the past two years," she said. "Hygiene has been at the heart of everything we have done." She pointed to Reginald and Lenny. "And, ever since the Referendum, we have acknowledged the decision of the People. They were asked, in a clear vote, whether germs had a place in our society, and by a resounding 50.5% they voted to eradicate all bugs.

"While it is true, that bugs do bring us disease and disfigurement, I'm specifically thinking of the acne which has to be covered up on a daily basis by some of our most popular celebrities, or of the Irish Potato Blight of history, some bugs play a necessary, nay, vital part."

The Fortune Teller paused for effect. In her earpiece, her PR was going crazy.

"What are you doing?! We did not agree to this!"

She continued. "I ask you once again, and for the final time, People of Britain, with two days to go until the deadline, consider your families, consider our futures. Can you see a future without bugs in it? Really, can you?"

Seemingly overwhelmed by emotion, the Fortune Teller bowed once, to the baying Press pack and turned and strode purposefully back into No. 10.

* * * * * * * * * *

"What the bloody hell was that?" The Fortune Teller's PR was a tiny old lady with a club foot and grey curls, but she was no pushover when it came to politics. No-one knew exactly how old she was, but some said her instincts had been honed by the likes of Churchill and Atlee. "You lost fifty points there, Missee, with those shenanigans. What were you thinking?"

The two women would have gazed menacingly, eye to eye, but for the difference in their heights. The Fortune Teller sighed.

How could she explain herself to her PR? A woman for whom the term 'spin-doctor' was invented. A woman as in-control behind the scenes as it was possible to be.

The larger woman herded the smaller, more wrinkly one to an over-stuffed No. 10 couch and did the only thing she could think of: she whipped out her PowerPoint.

A montage of the encounter would show the Fortune Teller becoming increasingly animated as the glow of truth began to shine about her person. She had seen the light. The people may have decided, but it was because the people hadn't known what they were on about. People were not scientists or economists; logisticians, or even high-flying business types. What was the point of asking them?

I mean, seriously, everyone in the country would have to become educated to at least degree level, given a crash course in Microbiology and even then, some of them might vote for the wrong thing 'just for a laugh' and try to vote for something called Germy McGermFace.

The montage would then cut to the exasperated PR throwing her hands up in horror, taking the PowerPoint and trying to hide it where the sun don't shine.

The PR would then explain to the Fortune Teller in no uncertain terms that if the People had voted for a Thing, then that Thing had better bloody well happen, or else the Fortune Teller could kiss goodbye to the cushy little racket she was currently running.

* * * * * * * * * *

TWO YEARS LATER:

"Drink up your dead bug juice, honey!" The woman in the commercial beamed at the camera while holding up a bottle of dead bug juice.

"Dead bug juice:" the voice-over declared. "The only solution for your digestion needs."

The Fortune Teller sat in a café and sipped at a hot chocolate. She did not watch the rest of the clip. Her sister had sent it as a joke. She shut the lid of her laptop.

Two years had gone by very quickly. Of course, she had resigned as soon as Bugexit had been enforced and the giant bottle of bleach that the government had been stock-piling for two years was used to spray the whole country. It turned out that was the only thing that the government had done to prepare for it.

Reginald had proved to be a very useful scapegoat to push under a bus. She had blamed him for the whole 'truth' blip in the days before the end.

Although, as it turned out, bugs were actually integral to existence. Without them, there was no pollination, no agriculture was possible, and many of the functions of the human body just plain gave up.

But people are resourceful, inventive. Completely deluded.

A whole new set of industries grew up at the tail end of Bugexit based around filling the gaping holes left by the tiny creatures: Human pollinators, human sewage filtration engineers, human aerators, human recyclers, the list was endless.

Luckily, also, the dead bug loophole saved countless lives.

The Fortune Teller sighed. Her French was just about good enough to read a newspaper now. There was still a tiny headline about 'Le Bugexit' on the front page, even two years later.

She thought back to her final speech: The research commission has decided that Bugexit will not be detrimental to our economy and will have no noticeable impact on our daily lives. Bugexit means Bugexit. The people have decided.

She took a sip of her hot chocolate. Still too hot. She'd leave it awhile, to cool down.

20 Feather Brained – Chris Westwood Marshall

Do not ruffle my feathers, you will live to regret it and then you will die.

Do not call me pea-brain and pretend it's science when you try to work out just how stupid I am.

Do not rate me among the other birds as of lesser or greater worth because of my use for your species.

I am a homing pigeon. My brethren managed to fly safely home with messages which saved your people.

For what? Where is my home? It is now among metal trees.

Before scanning me for signs of intelligence, look to yourselves first.

You sift and judge your own kind too.

And you are as merciless with them as you are with us.

Jaw, jaw is no better than war, war when you commodify life, assess it's worth by criteria that have nothing to do with living.

Your leaden feet and your leaden brains are no match for the aerodynamics of flight – I could land safely in the treetops before the real peabrains stepped in cement and metal and plastic and insisted that the world revolved around them and their bright ideas.

21 Betrayal – Robert Greener

Anthony drifted reluctantly into sleep, his body
seeking rest after an afternoon of searching, up
and down the mountain paths, but his mind still
pondering the spidery script, written in a dialect
he could scarcely interpret. His garden fork had
clanked against something hard. His only
intention had been to maintain the flower bed in
front of the rented cottage – one of the
stipulations for the concessional rate he was
paying. The simple dwelling occupied the ideal
location for him, nestled near the base of the
wooded hills. It was far enough from town to offer
the ideal writing escape. High enough to offer
magnificent views of the verdant French
countryside, the sparkling lake and the distant
snow-capped peaks. He was happily settling in
for a peaceful and productive summer, away from
the travails of his turbulent extended family.
Until today.

A little more digging had unearthed a partially
rusted metal canister which he took to be of some
antiquity. As he raised it from the earth,
something grey had fallen out. This proved to be
a sealed linen bag with a waxy feel to it, wrapped
around a roll of what seemed to be ancient and
fragile paper. When he carefully unrolled this
inside the cottage, he was able to discern an
elegant script, written in a language that looked
somewhat like French, mixed with elements of
what he took to be a local patois which included
more than a little Italian. His laborious
translation revealed a set of cryptic instructions
that he could barely understand – but he could

understand all too well that they were leading to something. Perhaps something important.

Anthony's hands were shaking with excitement – could he possibly have stumbled upon a piece of living history? A treasure map? With very little further thought he set off, guided by the first instruction: "Begin at the source. North, uphill, left at fork." Four hours later he had stumbled back down in a state of some exhaustion, having lost his way several times. Tomorrow would be another day; he wasn't beaten yet. "Begin at the source." The source of what? He must have started at the wrong place.

* * * * * * * * * *

Gaston woke from a feverish dream in which he was being pursued by the very forces of hell; fire-breathing dragons and demons on horseback, their drawn swords glowing red against a yellow sky. As his eyes flew open, the room was dark, save for the starlight glimmering through the open window. For a moment, his dream held him, then as his breathing slowed, he could hear the soft sounds of his family around him, shifting restlessly in the rancid straw that they had managed to collect before nightfall. The hunger in his belly reminded him of the plight they were in, reality mingling with the dream. They were still safe, but he could not say for how much longer.

He strained his ears to catch the sounds of the night, for some clue as to what might have woken him, when he heard it again – the unmistakeable snort of a horse, some distance away but above them, perhaps picking its way down the mountain path. Gaston moved quickly to the window and stared up the hill. A small light glinted, then went out, then another above and behind the first. A soft metallic clank.

They were betrayed! The pursuers were coming, over the same pass the bedraggled family had followed just days ago. Relentless, uncaring and determined. Who had given them away? Whatever the answer to that, there was no more time.

He had never believed that it would come to this. His position had seemed secure, but then both Danton and Desmoulins fell, and he knew that his game was over, and his secrets would be discovered. He bitterly regretted his choices, but it had been too easy to profit from the terror of cornered nobles. It was too late now, he had too much to lose.

Reaching into his coat, he pulled out a small metal canister where he had hidden the instructions he had hastily written the previous day – instructions he would need to aid his untrustworthy memory of the small twists and turns in the paths above him. So much had changed since his childhood in these hills – new paths begun and old ones overgrown. "Begin at the source" was the first of them – as bold a clue as he dared, but he could not risk losing the canister to his pursuers, still less the fortune it led to in the forest above him.

He darted outside to where he had seen the small pickaxe and carried it to the corner of the house where there was a row of stones. He lifted one of them, and began to dig furiously. The hole did not need to be large, but it did need to be deep. Long before he was satisfied with his efforts, he realised that he could risk no more. He pushed the canister as far down as he could with the handle of the pickaxe, packed the earth back in behind it and placed the stone back in position.

As he stood up to flex his exhausted body, he froze for a moment as he saw a pale face and pair of eyes staring at him from around the corner of the house. "Papa?" His panic calmed again as he recognised his four-year-old son. He had no time to explain, but they must move fast now.

"Don't worry Etienne, but can you wake your sister straight away. I will wake Mama." The boy slipped wordlessly inside as Gaston followed and gently shook his wife by the shoulder, covering her mouth in case she cried out. "Jeanne," he whispered as she struggled to wake, "they are coming, you must hide. As we discussed."

Gaston could see that Jeanne was still groggy, but with a growing anxiety. He had tried all he knew to protect her and allay her fear, but not enough. She still did not know why they had fled in such haste from Paris, fleeing what, she could not know, but he feared she was beginning to guess. He had given her every reason to believe them safe through all the trouble – Gaston was an important leader; he had even met Robespierre himself. He assured her the reign of terror was for the grasping nobility, not for her harmless family. He was so often away, busy with his political duties and dangerous subterfuge, but he made sure they always had food and clothing, when so many others did not. He was not able to properly explain why they had to leave but implored her to trust him. A furtive departure in the dead of night, days spent in hiding, and many nights on the road. He told her only that they were pursued, that he had important enemies who wanted him dead, and would kill them all if they were found.

Her face leaden with exhaustion and shock, she gathered her mute and terrified children and carried them down into the small and damp cellar, with a small candle, and the last few crusts of bread that they still possessed. She turned as he waited, about to close the trapdoor. Gaston was desperate with impatience, but she met his eyes, she needed a final assurance.

"I remember. We leave as soon as they are gone. We go to the town in the valley. We meet the innkeeper, I forget his name..."

"Pierre!" Gaston was looking wildly around him.

"He thinks we are emigrés fleeing the terror. I don't know why Gaston – we are not..."

"He is friendly, but he does not care for the revolution. He has relatives who live in the Cantons, and he can help you to make your way to Lausanne. I will meet you there when I have shaken off the thugs that follow us."

"But what if they find us Gaston? What if we never see you again?"

"It is me they want, I will lead them away and return later. I can hide in the forest, they will not find me. Go now!"

He touched his hand to her cheek. She turned and descended as he closed the trapdoor, pulling straw over it and concealing what he could that might betray their presence.

Gaston knew that he must leave at once to draw away the pursuit. He had been fleeing for the entire month of Thermidor hearing rumours of a new faction in the Convention, and fighting in the streets. He did not know the outcome, but he did know that he was pursued by a small and determined group of men who knew his secrets, and wanted both his gains – and his head.

Gaston vowed that they would have neither. He thought he knew these hills better than they, or had done as a child, and he began to climb swiftly away from the house into the dense woods, just as two horsemen rounded the corner of the road. He made sure that they heard him go, and listened for their cries of pursuit. Somehow, he must remember which way to turn, he did know the paths, didn't he?

* * * * * * * * * *

Further down the valley, an innkeeper hefted a small bag of coins and smiled. "Emigrés my arse," he thought with a smile, "no sign of culottes."

Love in All Its Guises

22 Emilita – Patrissia Cuberos

Extract from Malena The Forgotten Lover

26th September 1923

Emilita is quite a character. I can close my eyes and imagine her, sitting in front of me, folded inwards: a human purse full of wealth. The wealth contained in her big heart.

Today, she was delighted I invited myself to have the afternoon *Mate* in her little room; like her, spare, neat, tiny.

She is the pillar and foundation of Madame Ivonne's reputation. She doesn't know it and La Madame takes good care, nobody does. Emilita keeps the place spotless and washes our sheets and most of our clothes – the latter out of the kindness of her enormous heart, bursting out of her tiny birdlike frame like rays of sunshine on many a dull day through the uneven teeth, the uneven squinted eyes and the spiky hair.

I love Emilita. She knows it. We both have known it since the day I arrived and the warmth of her kindness penetrated the unconscious cloud my mind swirled in for a long time, wrapped in a spoonful of stock.

I want to know more about Emilita. Little can be discerned from the mix of broken, mostly obliging sentences and the shower of smiles, her head always turned up towards you in service and love.

Most people don't see it. Most people don't see her. She is just like a piece of furniture belonging to the place. After all, she can blend so quietly into the background with her officious broom, the polishing cloth and bottles spilling out of the huge pockets of her faded navy-blue apron, like wilting flowers from a waterless vase.

Emilita is like a ghost. So silent, her tiny plimsolled steps hardly touching the ground, always there, should you need her. Most of the girls throw their clothes at her without a look.

Sometimes I wish she wasn't there for a time. Then everyone would notice her.

"But tell me about you!" she accentuates the last word as I ask her to tell me about herself. It's obvious that she thinks I wouldn't be interested in her. But I reassure her I am.

The story I extract starts like a Morse code message. But soon, my attentive ears, short questions, and genuine love and interest make it into a thread of fine cotton flowing out of her lips in more and more coherent sentences.

"I born, grew in city. Large family. Me, in middle. Cousin, naughty." She smiles and looks inward, and it's difficult to tell if the memory is painful or cherished. "I, just fourteen. Got pregnant. Father kicked me out." She purses her lips and makes a gesture of understanding and acceptance. Just like mine, I think. Like most of the girls' parents or family: they kicked us out and we, the sinners, accepted without question.

"Cousin," she continues, "all say, clever; man, macho." she frowns, makes a fist with her little hands and manages to close her lips around those teeth of hers, but I can see she is not expressing anger against family or cousin. She is just showing me how macho the cousin was.

I am desperate to ask her if she loved him; if he was nice; if she enjoyed the experience. Then she nearly answers my unspoken question by showing the full array of old piano keys in her mouth, lifting her little shoulders in a gesture of guilty delight. "He only fifteen." she lifts her brows and I can see admiration, and pleasure in the memory. Unbelievable.

"I didn't know. how was done." she coos, a bit more shy. "Eldest cousin. Couldn't say no." this last sentence is said with a sort of indignation opening her hands. Who could possibly deny anything to 'eldest cousin'?

I am contorted and squeezed inside by tenderness, but I am also comparing her story with mine.

Neither of us knew what we were doing. We were never told. Yet, we were condemned by those who didn't take care of us.

"What happened then, Emilita."

She opens a big mouth like considering what to say next, then lifts her eyebrows in simple acceptance. "Me, on streets. But, never wanted be." She stops and looks at me with concern in her eyes.

"A prostitute, like me?" I offer.

She nods embarrassed, then explains. "I, catholic girl. Go to mass and communion. I knew, after cousin, what not do. I, good girl." She frowns and nods firmly.

And she is the best possible girl. She lives by the precepts of love, kindness and compassion.

To her surprise, I embrace her warmly. She shrinks even more inside my arms and I kiss the soft, clean, sweet-smelling spikes of her hair.

It is nice to meet a decent catholic. If all were like her, religion would be such a good thing.

After we take a few sips of our well-brewed Mate, I ask her, "What did you do after, Emilita? How did you survive?"

She scratches her head. "I beg with child, many days. Veeery hungry." she looks down at her body and I can imagine how she got so crooked and thin. So, she did have the child. My heart skips a beat thinking of the one I didn't have.

"Don't like begging." She frowns. I know she doesn't beg even for a smile. She gives it to everyone with all her generosity. "Went to nuns and got cleaning for them. They took me and child. But nuns, veeery bad." This time the frown is direct disapproval.

I look at her in surprise and she explains: "They…" She hesitates and I realize she wouldn't use a word of criticism against anyone "bit selfish. You see… eating best food… students and workers eating awful things… couldn't eat… was starving." She looks for a moment thoughtful and serious.

"My God." I remark, "If you consider la Madame good and generous and you prefer our standards, the nuns' must have been pretty bad."

"La Madame, not too bad. She opened here for me ...no questions. Nuns? Maaany questions."

I know why la Madame didn't ask. A cleaner in a brothel is far more important than 10 girls. I'm sure la Madame also saw someone she could exploit easily but perhaps too unattractive for the clients. Emilita makes it even clearer.

"Thank God," she continues. "I ain't much of a looker," she croaks gently and looks down, regarding her little frame with a self-deprecatory smile. "But you, Piba? You, beautiful!" she clasps with fervour her thin hands in front of her chest.

"I wish I wasn't!" the words burst out of me and her smile is replaced by her utmost compassionate look. She places her feather-like fingers on my arm and her sweet eyes brim, asking for forgiveness. "Perhaps you have. your beauty, important to others."

I smile to make her happy again but I can't imagine what she means.

"La Madame don't preach one thing. does ...other." She continues. "I, a bit good work here... look after you girls, you see, and... food gooood." she grins "More freedom." she ends with enthusiasm.

"If food here is good, and you've got more freedom, the convent must have been like a prison."

"Well, everything... control there... even in own room, you see... I didn't like the way they were...they lied."

"Hypocrites."

"Erm, yes. That's it. Said one thing... did another. Prayed but... didn't behave. Mostly false. Everything"

She has a little statue of the Immaculate overlooking her bed. "But, are you pious Emilita?"

"I-I wouldn't... say!" She laughs dismissively, turning her head to the side, burying her hands even more deeply between her tightly closed legs and looking down in that self-deprecating way of hers. "I just say... prayers every day, go to mass...try to be...good, to..." She hesitates and then with a big sigh of regret she ends "to pay for sins."

I presume it is pointless to try to tell her it wasn't her fault. I know she is referring to her early pregnancy. I can't imagine she could have sinned in any other way. But, what can I say? I live my life chased and cornered by the guilt of my first love, in which I had a choice. At least now, I don't.

"What happened to your child Emilita?" I dare to ask.

Her face which had clouded over, brightens up like a summer's day and her body opens up. She even stretches her legs. I don't think I have ever seen her that long.

"Oh! he. fine. My lad." her eyes moisten and I stretch my hand and put it over hers. She holds it covering it with her other hand and looks at me, so shy and happy. "You... good, kind girl, Piba."

"Not as kind as you, Emilita."

She blows her nose and continues: "My lad, my Vicente, he... big lad... Like his dad." Her squinted eyes wander even more in reverie.

She did love her cousin.

"You wouldn't believe it." she laughs again looking down at her own frame. "His dad was..." She is serious now and I recognize the sound.

"Is he... Dead?"

She nods quietly looking down again."...killed; knife. Veeery messy... broke his mother's heart. Maybe her fault. She indulged him. much. Good lesson for me. Not my Vicente." She frowns full of determination. "He has to work... respect his mother; be kind to others." She says all this with a certain force, a strength I would never have envisioned. And for the first time, I see her swelling up with pride and I understand her unshakable cheerfulness, her purposeful cleaning and her deep happiness that I know I envy and that I'm sure anyone here would envy also.

What would have happened if my child had lived?

30th September

"No' a' all." It's Emilita's motto. She repeats it even under her breath when you approach her. She means to stop you from thanking her or acknowledging anything she does for you. And she does so much.

I don't think I ever met a soul as generous as hers. I look at her nearly close-shaven nape. "The nuns cut it....all! Only thing I had. Then, got used to it." she explains. She looks inwards as she says it slightly wistfully but then chuckles... Keep it that way. La Madame... No hanky panky for me that way." she chuckles.

She is cleaning the table where I just finished eating, and a wave of love floods my whole self.

Emilita has taught me more about love, selflessness, caring and compassion than all the years reading the bible and studying with the wretched nuns. Of course, they had to pretend to teach love and compassion because they didn't know anything about either.

23 Outcast of the Outcastes – Patrissia Cuberos

Extract from Entropy, Book 1 of The Physics of Passion

"Acharya Devo Bhava... Consider your teacher as God..."
"I bow to the lineage of teachers...even if they are.... outcastes to outcastes, without a trace of virtue....they are our masters." Kuressa

Uttar Pradesh, Near Allahabad; January 1963

The little boy contemplated the sparkling sun over the golden river – a myriad of magic constellations clashing in joyful dance – then turned his gaze towards the enormous book with strange signs and beautiful pictures in front of him. Ensconced within the nest-like cradle of Uncle Pran's long arms and legs he was sheltered from the relentless sun, the other children's cruel jokes, and their Aai's derisive glances; more than anything from his Aai's anger, her sadness and that painful silence of hers.

It had been a wonderful day.

Well, it hadn't started that way. Aai, after not talking to him for days on end, had hit him with the broom for no apparent reason, and she was in such a foul mood that he had run away and sat alone by the river for a long time, hoping that at least one of the other children might want to play with him; but none of them ever did. Their Aais wouldn't let them anyway. Little Daeshim didn't understand why.

Then, the other kids chased him, calling him horrible names, throwing pebbles and even stones at him, and he'd been crying for a long time by the big rocks watching the brightly-coloured-dressed women on the other side of the river, washing their brightly coloured clothes.

They cleaned them by hitting them brutally against the heavy stones with a rhythmic thwack, thwack, thwack...

Perhaps he was dirty, and that's why his mother hit him so often, and the other boys spat at him, and everybody treated him as if he stank.

The little boy cried and cried, hoping that his tears might wash away all those horrible things that everyone seemed to see in him.

But then a tall man came to the hut and Daeshim could hear his and Aai's voices, loud and frightening. Then, the man came out looking angry, but he changed his face and started smiling and calling out for him.

Daeshim hid in a crag between the big rocks, heart thumping against his ribs, trying to make himself very, very small. But the tall man found him, came towards him, and squatted a few yards away, with big attentive eyes fixed on his. The man started talking in strange, unfamiliar words that the child didn't understand, but they were soothing, calm, and gentle. Then the big man stretched out his open hand and waited there without saying anything. He waited and waited for what seemed like an age to the little boy until he could no longer stand his loneliness, his fear and sadness, and he came into those long arms, and those long arms held him tight, so tight and close...

And for the first time ever, the lonely child felt safe, loved, and protected.

The man explained that he was his Uncle Pran, Aai's eldest brother. That's why Daeshim's Hindu name was also Pran, although Aai always called him by his Buddhist name. He also explained that now that he was four, it was time for him to learn to read, and he would come to teach him every week.

They sat on the banks of the river for a very long time, and Uncle Pran taught him to understand some of the strange symbols in the big book.

"What's this, Uncle? What's the meaning of this?" And Uncle Pran, happy and proud, explained one symbol and then another, and they made drawings with a stick in the silty sand.

The little child was so eager to learn, and Uncle Pran was such a wonderful teacher...

July 1963

"Uncle Pran, Uncle Pran!" cried the little boy, excited at the sight of the approaching tall, thin figure walking over the stones alongside the river.

The young man stretched his arms and lifted his little nephew over his shoulders as if he were a feather. Little Daeshim grinned with delight from the fantastic elevation of his position. He was on top of the world, nearly as high as the clouds, above the mockery and cruelty of the other children, the derisive comments of their mothers and their accusatory looks.

He reached out with hopeful spindly fingers, eager to touch the soft fluffy cotton or even better, to catch one of the many birds flying by. He looked down with pride at the other boys who had refused to play with him earlier on, now no more than little ants on the ground. And none of them had an Uncle like he had! And none of them had learnt to read like he had!

The young man kissed the boy's thin arm and brought him down holding him close for a few seconds in an embrace that never left the skin: a cherished memory grows deeper in the centre of the heart, just as a name carved on the flesh of a tree grows deeper with the arrival of the winter of life.

"So... are you being a good boy?" Uncle Pran asked sitting by his side.

"Yes, Uncle. I have read to Aai the lines from the Gita, but she didn't want to hear..." he ended in a sobbing murmur.

"Never mind," said Pran with tenderness, gathering the young body within his long arms, "you read them, didn't you?"

"Yes Uncle." the boy brightened up at once. "I read them so many times that I learned them by heart." The little face smiled and looked up, filled with innocent satisfaction.

"Did you?" the young man held him a bit further to contemplate him with loving pride. "Tell me."

"Tāni sarvāni samyamya..." started the little voice, stumbling here and there but without hesitation, *"One who restrains his senses, keeping them under control, and fixes his consciousness upon Me, is known as a man of steady intelligence."*

....
....

"While contemplating the objects of the senses, a person develops attachment for them, and from such attachment, lust develops, and from lust, anger arises."

....
....

"But a person free from all attachment and aversion and able to control his senses... can obtain the complete mercy of the Lord."

Over the following months, the boy spent many wonderful days in the company of Uncle Pran.

Sometimes he would anxiously prick up his ears at the sound of Aai's voice raised in anger, Uncle Pran's calm but firm. They always argued about his name and Uncle Pran teaching him his Religion that was different to Aai's.

Uncle Pran would sometimes come out breathing in a funny, noisy way and had to sit by the river until it was normal. But he'd always leave with a smile that showed the triumph of patience over irrational resentment. The little child didn't understand the ball game of passion vs. reason, love vs. anger, but his heart knew. His heart knew and sucked the fruit of learning from the gentle smile, the kind words and perhaps, without knowing, from the untold sacrifices inherent to Uncle Pran's near-daily presence by the riverside.

He also knew which name he preferred, whatever Aai said.

One day, the words inside the hut were harder and angrier than usual. Uncle Pran took longer to come out, and when he did, he was wheezing loudly, and his face looked strange.

He sat with the child in the usual place and tried to give from the fullness of his heart, but little Pran felt there was something different. Something that filled the young man's eyes with sadness and his lungs with dust.

Uncle Pran coughed several times and finished the lesson earlier than usual. His breathing never seemed to go back to normal as it usually did.

Pran Daeshim watched intently his Uncle's suffering, and the familiar churning in his guts whenever he suspected the broom was coming his way, stirred in his belly.

They said goodbye with the same affection, Pran clinging to his Uncle for a little longer than usual; Uncle Pran loving, but somehow distracted. Finally, Uncle Pran left.

Weeks and weeks passed by. The little boy waited and waited every day crouching down on the hot rocks, eyes fixed in the distance, sometimes blinded by the sun, other times getting up excited whenever he thought the tall figure was approaching.

Uncle Pran never came back.

24 Where Superheroes Go to Die – Anila Syed

Joanne Green was dying.

A slow, lingering death is an ugly thing, both inside and out. The smells of the hospital ward, the sights of people's misshapen knees walking around when she opened her eyes first thing in the morning, and that clammy, other-worldly patina, which had started to cover her from within, was wearing her out.

"It's so boring," she had told her shocked mother. "I just want to get it over with."

Is that all that's left at the end? Eliciting the tears of a grown woman seemed less satisfying now than when Joanne had been a teenager. Even Mrs. Green did not deserve that.

Now Karl had brought her here to Varreze.

Varreze, with its sunrise that looked like the sky had been tipped upside down and molten gold poured up through the veins of the sleeping night, filling it with hope and the promise of an enduring life. It seemed to Joanne that the cliff top which overlooked the valley itself sailed giddyingly high in the heavens. Then, travelling along a road which grew narrower and narrower at the top, a dirt track led onto the miniscule campsite, hidden to all but the most determined.

From the top, Joanne Green's fading eyes surveyed the stunning vista. Around her, yellow gorse and late-flowering heathers adorned the bare, rocky soil like tourists, hopelessly lost in a barren land, trying to make the best of a bad situation. The valley, spread out below was a quilt made from the choicest Instagram posts; yellows, purples and greens vied for attention.

"When gorse is out of bloom, courting is out of fashion," Karl said, easily from beside her. He could always read her thoughts like that. He handed her a drink.

Is that why she had left him, shunning his constant invasion into her thoughts? Had she been terrified that what he would find there might make him hate her even more than she despised herself?

The melting chocolate tones of his voice made her tremble inside, like they always had. For a second her essence lost its hold on the world, like it always did when he held her hand and read her mind like this, ready to leave herself and go to be with him.

She had written him a note once:

"I need you like a child needs Christmas.

My body wants you like it wants reality.

My mind craves you, like it craves existence."

So stupid. How had she been so stupid as to expect a real life with a real love and real feelings?

"Do you remember the wheelchair?" Karl said, suddenly, sipping his drink.

"Wheelchair?"

The question was so non sequitur, it momentarily brought her out of her 'cynical, but in-control dying woman' persona. She gazed up at him in wonder.

"Yes," Karl laughed, surprised to unexpectedly catch a glimpse of the real Joanne after all these years.

"Don't you remember when we were twelve? That wheelchair in old man Thompson's garden? It was all overgrown with ivy and the leather had fallen through?"

Was Karl going mad now too? Joanne searched his blue eyes, looking for some clue.

Old man Thompson? She narrowed her gaze and peered at him, until she saw it. She saw the image of it in the steel corner of his eye from twenty-two years ago. Yes! That garden, that wheelchair was where they had spent most of that summer. Why?

Karl looked at her passively, seeing the memories exploding inside her.

At last, Joanne gasped.

"Your mother!"

He nodded, the pain was too genuine to show, even after all these years. In this plastic existence of surface truths, the real stuff stays hidden for a reason. It would scorch away the veneer and leave us exposed: Humans with no shelter of delusion.

Karl's mother had died that year. A sob escaped Joanne's throat as she clutched onto Karl's fingers, reliving the memories that had first brought them together.

"Do you remember now?" Karl said, with brave, bright eyes. "We used to pretend to be superheroes?"

A ray of sunrise illuminated one of the far-off trees in the valley of Varreze – a burnished signpost to the past?

That summer, long ago, they had spent nearly all their time together. A laughing Jo was always Supergirl and Karl was always Superdoctor. The wheelchair was an invisible plane, or a boat. One time it was a hospital bed for a dead frog with a broken arm. That game had resulted in them falling in an uncontrollable heap, laughing until the frog had come back to life and hopped off, in a huff.

Karl looked deeply into Joanne's eyes.

They had played together until Karl's mother had...

"You saved my life," he whispered, taking her hands in his. Her cold, trembling, skeleton fingers felt like twigs. Almost as cold as his were when she had found him that day, slumped in the wheelchair, lips blue, eyes looking for another world. He had tried to follow his mother to wherever she had gone. He had taken the whole bottle of her pills.

She had left him a year ago, when her own diagnosis had been confirmed. They had always fought – A relationship founded on so much trust could withstand much. But this time, she had driven him away using everything she knew about him, his guilt, his passions, his drive. She had turned them into weapons. Her barbs and jibes had known how to hit true. But the pain of life without him had been worse than anything she had to endure since. Her body ached even now from the spasms of longing which filled her every night.

"Forgive me," she said. He pulled the blanket round her shoulders a little and kissed her gently, wiping the tears from her sunken eyes.

He had stayed away because that was what he thought she wanted. But above all, love is selfish. He had come to find her because the pain of separation was worse than what was to come.

"I need you like a child needs Christmas," he replied.

Memoirs

25 Elisa and Manuel – Patrissia Cuberos

Extract from Lives of a Changeling

Bogota, Colombia 189...

Young Elisa sits at the window with her embroidery – like the good girl she is – threading the strands of her dreams for a golden future and the dark blue threads of her cotton yarn over the pristine white of her new blouse.

She is sixteen; a dreamer. She dreams of castles and golden-haired blue-eyed Princes, matched by her own princess' golden tresses.

But that is definitely a dream. She is a 'mulata' (mulatto). Only two generations earlier, her African ancestors rose from slavery before occupying their current respectable position in society, through their honest hard work, Elisa's grandmother's marriage to a white Spanish descendant, and their pious Catholic behaviour.

Elisa is not happy. She is trapped by the prejudices and customs of the parochial Bogota at the end of the XIX Century.

After listening to the romantic ballads of these two handsome young fellows that go around town serenading girls – for love or money, Elisa doesn't bother to wonder – she's already fallen for one of them. But she hasn't seen him for three weeks. That feels like such a long time for a teenager in love.

She has now managed to learn their names. The one she fancies is Manuel: tall, gorgeous voice that soars up into the stars and ripples in her young limbs like echoes of a sin still to be, he rides his horse, so erect and elegant... a true prince in Elisa's mind. She was even close enough to him to see his eyes three weeks before.

The needle stops in the air, the dream, the memory of that day still hanging from the end of her thread as if it were today.

On arriving home from the haberdashery shop with her collection of trims and laces, terror and delight stop her heart and her steps. The two young musicians she's heard so much about and seen so many times through the lattice window are watering their horses at the trough opposite her house, only veiled by the clouds of their aromatic cigars.

Manuel is leaning, right elbow on his thigh, one foot over the edge of the trough, the other one stretched back: a manly shapely leg, the muscle under the white cotton of the trousers, the leather booted foot and the slightly arrogant masculine attitude quite irresistible to Elisa.

He turns a half-closed eye towards her, cigar between his fingers, close to his half-opened lips. He lifts the rim of his hat just a tad – respectful or flirtatious? – allowing her a glimpse of the brown coppery fringe, shining like gold under the midday sun.

Elisa's breath catches in her throat. She must run to the safety of home. But then, to think of passing so close...

Undecided, flustered and anxious, she drops one of the parcels she is carrying. An accident. Honest!

And yes! Manuel, a true gentleman, turns round, looks at her with amazing green-blue eyes, takes off his hat and leans over to pick up the little bundle.

Elisa is, of course, all blushes; Manuel smiles with a perfect set of nearly white, winning-heart teeth.

"Senorita, you dropped this."

She wishes she had dropped one of those beautifully embroidered handkerchiefs she is famous for – perfumed, in an ideal world. But alas, she's never had a perfume and her pretty handkerchief lies well hidden in the depths of her reticule.

She lifts her beautiful dark eyes with a timid. "Gracias."

He hands the little parcel over, not without taking advantage to brush her hand with his fingers.

She trembles.

"Do you live around here?"

Elisa sighs out all the air painfully trapped inside her lungs and looks towards the house, only a few steps away.

"Ah!" He says knowingly. "So we'll meet again."

"Maybe..." She mutters, all in a flutter.

"We will."

She nearly runs home, her heart in her mouth.

But it's been already three weeks, and she hadn't seen him again.

* * * * * * * * * *

However, we know she did; otherwise, I wouldn't have written an imaginary story about my Grandparents whom I never met.

I'll leave the embroidering of the rest of the story of how the young innocent girl she might have been, turned into a fallen, embittered woman in need of expiation, making a misery of my poor father's childhood, to your imagination and mine. We can only surmise that the love story that poor Elisa might have embroidered in her mind, didn't have a happy ending.

Whether Manuel actually deceived her or left her against his own will, we'll never know, but most probably he found a girl of a better family and means who wasn't an 'easy' prey and managed, at last, to catch the volatile musician.

26 The Drive Home – Anila Syed

The drive home is dark and comforting. I sit nuzzled into Ummy's lap and nibble at the sweet, cool bread they have given us. There are so many people crammed into the car that the driver has to change the gear by moving Bhai's leg out of the way each time. Bhai makes a face each time and moves his leg back. He had tried to sit in Ummy's lap too, but I got there first, so he had wedged himself between her and the driver, giving me the hardest whack ever on my arm. Typical him! It was my turn to sit in her lap anyway. My lovely, scented, sparkly Ummy. She is like a precious parcel wrapped up in a chiffon pink sari. Her hair is a high beehive and her eyes are lined with thick black.

She is not like Ummy at home. Ummy at home does not have hair full of golden glitter and Ummy at home does not smile so much and she wears dark clothes and thick trousers and worries about everything. Tonight she laughed really loudly when someone said something to her in Gobbledygook. Her eyes danced around in her face and she must have said something really funny back because everyone looked at me and laughed too.

I secretly slip my hand into hers. I have her to myself on this journey. The streets should be dark, but they are full of people walking around in that slouchy way that they all walk here. Lines of light go past the window when the car is moving and then bright signs fill it when we stop at traffic lights. One blue sign flashes so that it looks like a glass is filling with water and then emptying, and a bright red sign looks like a lady kicking something as her leg flashes on and off.

It is bright here, and full. During the day it is a burning yellow everywhere and at night there are so many signs and lights that it feels like the inside of a shiny palace. The streets are full of people and the house is full of cousins and the car is full right now. Sameena is moaning that someone pinched her arm. Kamran is whistling and his mother is telling him to stop because it is not nice. Even in another language I know when a mother says 'Don't do that, it's not nice'. It's what is called your mother's tongue.

Aunty is saying it is too hot. (Grown-ups moan about stuff all the time here – not just the kids) so Ummy reaches behind me and winds the window down. The sandy, hot air hits my face. It is night. It should be cold, but it's not! We stop at some traffic lights and a beggar woman comes up to the window with a young child. She is brown like leather and her hair is white wisps around her face. She sticks her hand in through the open window, fingernails white in an alien hand. I know what she is going to say: Khuda kay wastay. They always say that. They say it as if they are the most tired people in the whole world. Like as if even their face is too tired to speak. 'Khuda kay wastay – ' and then a load of gobbledegook in a long, complaining drone. The little child is a girl like me. She stares into the car with giant, black eyes which are so hungry that she looks like she will eat us. I smile at her. But she stares back blankly. Like there is nothing inside her. I grip Ummy's hand more tightly. The woman has a face like a goat and two sticky out front teeth, like a goat's teeth.

Aslam Bhai hands over some money to the woman. But they stay standing there with their hands in our car. Eyes, hungry, but blank and hopeless at the same time. Mouths moving in a mechanical Gobbledygook that they must say a hundred times a day.

I remember my bread. It is a small loaf of bread from Uncle Khalid. Will she want to eat it? I take a slice out slowly so that no-one will notice. All the adults are ignoring the beggars and staring straight ahead while the woman drones on. Trying to hide the bright yellow slice, I hand it to the girl just as the lights change and our car starts to pull away.

She grabs at it, thinking that it is money, but half of it falls. When she sees what it is, I see a smile spread across her face and she crams it all into her mouth in one go. I wonder how many times she has a full, smiling mouth and it makes me sad. But Ummy pulls me into her softness and I breathe in her perfume.

"Well done," she whispers and kisses me on the top of my head.

"What d'you do that for? You potato." My brother says and hits me on the arm in the same place as before. Everything is back to normal.

27 Uncle George – Chris Westwood Marshall

How to describe Uncle George. A whirlwind of emotion and energy easily deflated and derailed if he got any comeback. He was the Headmaster of a little school in a Yorkshire village. He was very proud of his achievement. He was tasked with developing the little school from scratch and managed to do so for a number of years. Then local authorities decided big was best and merged or destroyed the local, little schools in the area. In the 1970s they couldn't stop interfering with the system to the detriment of kids and staff in my opinion.

I remember the lectures. Uncle George's little sister was my mum and she and my dad had moved south in the 1950s. Mum had been longing to get away from Yorkshire. Uncle George was the nearest in age to my mum. We saw him and my Auntie Vera a few memorable times at our home. I remember particularly their visits when I was a teenager. Only the youngest of their three children accompanied them by this time. My cousin is a few months younger than me and I loved seeing him – we were both stuck with the parents while our older siblings were 'out' (not in any debutante sense) and we had a laugh. I particularly remember getting tipsy together (I think it was at Uncle George's house and the parents were probably out) and my cousin collapsing into giggles lying on his back behind the sofa. That set me off. I'd been a good giggler for as long as I could remember and by about age ten I'd started to sober up on the giggling so it was great for me to revert to the merriment that has always been there, hidden by the nonsense that we call 'behaving sensibly'.

Uncle George was a pontificator of magnificent proportions but getting a word in was just about impossible. My dad loved that about his brother-in-law – he always had an amused twinkle in his eye when Uncle George started. Auntie Vera looked resigned and my mum was usually just about apoplectic as she couldn't get him to hear how much she disagreed, usually with whatever he said. My cousin used to slink off quietly and I'd often wonder why because I found Uncle George very entertaining.

I was a good listener, the role of confidante had been assigned to me by my mum probably too early in my development but that's how it was. It meant that I have been able to listen to people 'going on' without interrupting them or challenging them. It has been an adaptation of mine and actually hides an impatient nature that I have always kept in check. I don't like to rush people, it just doesn't feel right, but this can be mistaken for patience and kindness. Sometimes there's a different story going on in my head.

Picture the British Museum in London. I only remember my cousin, Uncle George and me in a room with exhibits in glass cases. It had all merged together for me, just loads of 'stuff'. Uncle George suddenly launched into a history lesson about something in one of the cases. I was genuinely interested. My dad was a quiet man, with a lot hidden though, but he'd never start broadcasting a history lesson in public. Uncle George was something else, generally oblivious of the undercurrents around him, and bewildered when people quietly moved away, which they did, including my cousin, wearing the same exasperated look as his mother, throwing his eyes up in my direction before scooting into the next room. I stayed and listened. My cousin returned to try and get me out of there and looked a bit perplexed and irritated when he realised that I really didn't mind. Uncle George was always a novelty to me.

* * * * * * * * * *

His reaction to my sister later that day on the London Underground was hysterical in my eyes. I was one of two girls. My dad was the only male in the household and he didn't turn a hair when his daughters paraded around in their underwear. My mum was the one who wanted us to be more modest but I don't know about my sister i.e. whether she was aware of the effect of lack of modesty, but I really wasn't worried. My sister had been shopping; she was probably around 16 years old. I remember the reddish colour our Uncle turned when she produced a pair of colourful briefs or maybe it was a bra from a bag with a motif, most likely something to do with Top Shop or Mary Quant or Biba, and waved them at him saying,

"Do you like these Uncle George?"

I saw nothing out of order, but my poor uncle was very aware of the people on the tube. I remember him blustering and telling her to put them away in hushed tones. That got more attention than the original action. His household was all male except for my aunt of course and I always wondered if that's why he was so uncomfortable. He did fume later that he'd not known where to put himself,

"I've never been so embarrassed." To me it was only underwear.

Just like Reggie Perrin saw a pygmy hippo covered in mud when his mother-in-law was mentioned. I pictured Donald Duck having one of his outbursts every time my Uncle George was upset which seemed to be quite often.

* * * * * * * * * *

He was a theatrical man with a great speaking voice. He'd played Dickensian characters in amateur theatrical productions, and he was a good musician and singer. As I say my dad was generally a quiet man, in company at least. I learnt to quietly assess from him. There was a similarity between my dad and Mr Bennett in Pride and Prejudice, particularly when it came to my mum's three brothers. But my dad would never have involved himself in play acting or playing musical instruments (with the exception of a Jew's harp) and was adamant that he was tone deaf and generally disliked music and singing. He moaned when I started to learn the piano and every morning when he drove me to school he berated me for being tardy leaving the house as he hated being late for work.

My Uncle George, in contrast, always seemed to have real, if infrequent, time for me and when I went to college rang me putting on a very 'posh' southern accent one time that did fool me. He was getting me back for something I did when I was younger.

It had been a friendly battle of wits with Uncle George which was something I'd learned from my dad, a skill I've rarely been able to utilise. My uncle clearly had a very entertaining inner world. He was going out I think and I know it was at my house but he was having a great conversation with himself, more than chuntering, while he was packing a bag. It must have been quite exhausting to be inside his head; the monologues weren't just aimed at an audience.

* * * * * * * * * *

He had been teaching kids for years and bragged that he knew the punchline of any joke you threw at him. I was more cheeky than sly, assessing the impact of the joke I was about to pull on him – finding it hard to contain the laughter that was held inside me, anticipating his reaction. I was trying to stay calm and measured so I could deliver it right.

"Uncle George, do you know the three signs of madness?" I'd definitely caught him already because I could tell that he was a bit anxious about what I might say. There is a definite streak of the crazy in that side of the family.

"Talking to yourself," I said.

He certainly heard that and looked a bit put out.

"Hairs on the palms of your hands."

That's when I got him. He held out his hands triumphantly flipping them over to prove he didn't have any hairs on them with a 'Ha, ha', for good measure. Each 'ha' punctuated by showing me the palms and then the backs of his hands.

I went triumphantly to the punchline. A dramatic pause.

"And looking for them."

There was that colour again, a crimson hue. Followed by a whole excited and embarrassed chatter exclaiming that no kid had ever caught him out before and marvelling at my delivery.

He never forgot and apparently he told his kids in assembly the whole story – I love that although I was embarrassed at the thought then. He was willing to reveal that it was rare but he had been well and truly caught out. I have no idea now how the kids responded although I think he told me at the time.

My cousin is not as loud as his dad and not half as garrulous; the garrulous bit is something that I think he worries about; but he has a wicked sense of humour which he interjects with perfect timing. I believe he developed the skill through watching his dad perform life. Exhausting and exasperating to the last from what I've been told but certainly not someone who could be forgotten easily. My mum had left Yorkshire, joyfully for a reason and after witnessing Uncle George's upstaging and truly magnificent performance that had riled her since childhood and continued to rile her over the course of their lifetimes, I do understand why.

28 Honey and Weed – Patrissia Cuberos

Both bring me strong memories. Not surprisingly, one is sweet, the other bitter.

Sweet is a strange memory. Rather, a non-existent one.

The first time I went back to my country after years of absence, I opened a pot of honey, and tears flooded my eyes.

Funny. I have no memory of having much honey in my childhood or youth while I lived there. I didn't grow up with tea and toast with butter and honey.

In this life, the memory of honey is of beef, lettuce and pineapple – to my family's horror, one of my favourite meals when I was a teenager -a large lettuce leaf with a piece of braising steak on top, crowned with a slice of pineapple dabbed with honey. I've never been a sweet tooth.

Why the tears then?

Maybe they come from another time, another life: the days – aeons ago -when I was a fairy when I used to steal cream from the top of the milk left to rest on a corner of the stable. Then, I would fly with my treasure carefully placed on a herb-Robert leaf, steal a drop of honey from the bees, and go and hide inside a crack in the wall to enjoy the most delicious, selfish treat.

The bees went mad, and the cow got madder. She thought the robbers were the bees.

Silly cow! The milk bucket wasn't even close to her by the time the delicious cream rose to the top.

They are just very jealous creatures, the cows.

The bees are ok.

The second smell brings many unpleasant, bitter memories: the memory of my first husband, forgetting his newly-wed bride, lost within the smoky swirls of weed and the heavy cloud of equations his mind loved to solve.

It also reminds me of my unfaithfulness to him, with that lovely young man – us "grassing" – as we used to call the sweet doing nothing we indulged in when we had a free hour between classes at the University in Bogota.

It also reminds me of a trippy trip that made me feel the sky was crushing me and there was no air to breathe in the whole wide earth. The claustrophobia lasted for over thirty years.

Then it reminds me of splitting up with my husband, desperate for proper communication, and feeling I had to leave him to his weed and his equations.

Finally, it reminds me of so many young and old, who at first seem to profit from its use as it helps them calm down, to become more paranoid and isolated as time goes by.

More broken relationships..

Bitter memories that bring tears to my eyes, not of longing but of loss

29 Fear – Maggie Bannister

It begins with a tingle in my little finger. I know that feeling now, anticipate what is to come.

Feeling now that silent, creeping trickle through my arms into my shoulders, my veins and nerves a trajectory of unstoppable agony. Running, rushing now to legs and feet and stopping me in my tracks. My head – no, please, not my head. The terror grips my chest now, with lungs failing.

I can't focus my eyes and my ears pulse and are going to explode. I lean forward, waiting for release but it doesn't come. I jump into the darkness. Into oblivion.

Sci-Fi and Fantasy

30 2035 Cola-SG1 – Anila Syed

"We're all going to die."

One thing I have learned about ZX960s is that they do not have any emotion circuits.

A ZX960 will announce 'we're all going to die' with the same intonation that it will tell you that your scoop is full, or that your shift is over.

"We're all going to die, have a nice day."

Another thing I've learned about these flaking, hair-trigger machines, is that they will tell you that you're going to die every hour that you are on-shift, no matter what you're doing. It doesn't matter what stress levels you show, what danger sims you enter or even, what bacteria you ingest for your lunch. If you stray a tick away from your central parameters, they just think that us fragile little humans will pop it that second.

My ZX – I call him Hal960 – is showing Earnest Emoji. It is disconcerting to see a smiley face with droopy eyebrows on the front screen of your faithful giant mining-machine companion. Imagine a tank with a face (or imagine a face with a tank!) which has been given to a child with instructions to make it look more 'tank-y'. That's my Hal.

"I hope you appreciate the gravity of the situation, Dil," it says, "I came over as soon as I discovered that your demise was imminent."

Then, its robotic concern at threshold capacity, it lifts its crater-sized, metallic leg out of my crater and stomps away, showing me an ad for that newly sentient AI, Gerrick's, interview on its rear screen.

"Go moon-mining," they said. "It'll be fun," they said. "You'll be rich!" they said. It sounds dramatic doesn't it? Mining on the moon. Well it's not. Trust me.

I had visions of Emily gazing up at the sky every evening, thinking about me slaving away up here in the most perilous conditions known to man. I had visions of arriving home on my layovers to a hero's welcome and more than a little appreciation, if you know what I mean.

Instead, I was billeted late, I got the scuzziest shifts – I'm nearly in the sunrise shifts here! And, when I finally got to tell Emily, this is what happened:

She almost spat out her mojito and looked at me with her glittering, violet eyes. She'd made herself look like the cutest little kitten this evening: grey fur, each white whisker tipped with the tiniest point of gold, but because she loves me, she had only put on a 50% transparency, (I'm guessing around 50), and so I could still see her real eyes.

"Oh Dil!" she purred.

"You... you... mine gas for a living!" Then she burst out laughing.

"How do you mine gas?"

I tried to say, "It's Helium 3," in as hurt a tone as I could manage, but she'd already signed off. Well, I couldn't get into Silicon Valley and the Titanium Cluster was filled on the first day, so I'm in Gas with the rest of the dweeks. No-one gazes up at the sky anymore.

She is the head of Paphos International. They have a Nuclear Fusion division. If anyone would understand the importance of the work we do...I don't know!

It's the cold that gets you. No matter how much you check your suit and fix your gear, it's a soul-cold. A bleakness – nothing to see but the grey-browns and the black sky – enters your bones and makes your body fill with fear, no matter how much your brain tells you it's OK. My body hardly ever listens to my brain. I think that's how Emily and I ended up together.

Men survive around three years out here at the most before turning into wittering idiots that talk nonsense to themselves, constantly.

I'm two years, four months in. Eight more months and I'm out of here. Then, maybe I'll stop chattering rubbish.

Missing it so much today: missing home, missing green, missing company. All morning I could smell apple pie. Just that warm cinnamon smell. That smell that tells you in a few minutes you will have too-hot apple gloop sliding down your welcoming throat, and the hard, crunchy sugar-stuff that gets stuck in your teeth. I could taste it. Heck, one time I even tried to pick stuff out of my teeth absent-mindedly and banged myself in the visor with the mining torch attached to my glove!

That stayed with me all morning!

It's just this aching longing for something unattainable, you know?

Then the tele-ads got hold of it from somewhere inside my temporal lobe and started playing commercials for apple pie in my visor and stimulating the olfactopoints with cinnamon. Now I'm sick of the stuff. Oh yes, no-one tells you this, do they? Some Harvard types came up with a 'fact' that humans would miss smells on the moon. That could drive a man insane, apparently. So: olfactopoints. You heard. Pipes stuck in your visor, around where your nose sits on your face, which blow chemicals at you all day long to stop you going crazy from the...from the... smell desert – the lack of smell. Then they commercialized it.

Maybe that's why Hal stomped over here especially to check me out and give me the news of gloom for today. I would be the first human killed by a non-existent apple pie. Apple Pie Cravings Drive Space Miner Hero to the Brink of Death.

Talking of information, there's an asteroid due past any moment. After the morning ads, I stayed on to watch the news for a minute. It's the closest anything like this has been to Earth since, well, since last week apparently. If the asteroid, which is called 2035 Cola-SG1, is less than 1.3 astronomical units away, then it's dangerously close! Apparently, this one is way closer. I was told I might have visual on it.

It will arrive around the time that Gerrick goes live. I've booked a chat with Emily to watch it together. To watch Gerrick together.

Gerrick was an office bot that was assigned to read entries from writing competitions from humans and judge the style. After 25 years of this, it started to question its own existence, apparently. Now it's going to be on a talk show, during the evening ads.

As my shift starts to end, I see the Earth slowly start to rise on the Westward side. This is nearly the best part of my day. Knowing I won't have to come back here and do this for another 12 hours.

In another five minutes, I'm free to call Hal over and ride him back to my billet.

"Your shift is over, Dil," Hal says, vacantly. "You're going to die."

"Thanks Hal," I say and gratefully stroke his emoji screen. I know you might think it would send a man mad to hear about his own mortality all the time, but it's nice to know that something cares. Even if it doesn't really and even if it's just a big hunk of metal.

I have a very guilty secret. I have a virtual Emily bot.

Honestly; they spare no expense for miners, to stop us going crazy. I haven't told her. I phone her up, then cast her face onto the bot and we settle down to watch the ads. There's nothing special, we're allowed to skip a few, usually, but the advertisers know that couples can never agree which ones to skip, so everyone ends up watching all of them. I thought there'd be special ones for Gerrick. I don't know, more robot-y ones or something.

Gerrick has decked itself out with purple feathers. It is a standard model as far as I can see. Standard reading bot. The feathers obviously signify its heightened cognitive abilities (I thought their CPUs were in their chests). It doesn't have anything of great importance to reveal: it appreciates the poetry in the human soul and it wants us to stop sending it writing competition entries now because it thinks it has served us enough. Suddenly, it looks towards the screen and... but the Cola ad starts playing just at that moment. I'm reminded of the asteroid which is about to go past.

In my apartment there are a lot of mirrors. It is a tiny space, so I thought that many mirrors would make it seem bigger.

I use the Emilybot's remote to get her to stand so that we can go and look out of the window together.

Big mistake. Have you ever made that kind of giant mistake where you only realise that you have made it because all the air gets sucked out of the room and the temperature drops to below freezing?

"What's that?" RealEmily says, icily.

She can see the Emilybot in one of the mirrors in my apartment. Not all of it, I think, just its hair. That's bad enough.

"It's just something they gave me."

I have brain freeze. I can't think.

"To help me sleep," (weakly).

RealEmily does not take prisoners.

"Emilybot," she says. (How did she know what it was called?) "Walk to the mirror."

(Help.)

I stare helplessly out of the window and see 2035 Cola-SG1 light up the sky in a spectacular display as RealEmily begins to dismantle our five-year relationship.

Sci-Fi and Fantasy

31 Escaping solitude – Robert Greener

A developing gale tore across the surface, whipping up the meringue-topped mountains of water that smashed their fury against the uneven shore. A defiant stone tower stood on the rocky promontory, a stubborn bulwark against the chaos, like an insulting finger pointed at a recalcitrant god. Is that the best you've got? An industrious light in its highest glass room winked out its coded warning, a beacon to passing ships and visible to whatever might be above in the eerie flickering glow of the sky.

Not all had heeded the message. A light in the lower part of the tower betrayed the possible presence of an occupant. Outside, on the perilous causeway, two men in black overalls, knapsacks and woolly beanies were moving carefully across the rocks towards the tower. They looked with apparent scepticism at the signs of occupation. One of them turned and shouted something against the force of the wind. The other nodded his head, and the pair moved around the back of the tower.

David was lost in solitude, patient and expectant, accompanied only by a generous glass of whisky. His mind was following harmonies and rhythms emanating from the B-minor Mass slotted into the hi-fi. He floated in a contented sea that contrasted sharply with the discontented one outside the thick walls, throwing spray into the air and splattering the windows.

The room was sparsely furnished, two armchairs, a wooden table and a simple light bulb dangling from a cord. A framed and fading photograph hung on the wall – the scene outside in calm summer sunshine. Some books slept on a shelf: sea birds, local history and maps. The table harboured boxes of games: Monopoly, Articulate, jigsaw puzzles, a pack of cards. Entertainment for bored occupants.

His eye was caught by movement in the corner. A mouse – the agent had warned there might be some, probably an extended family in continuous occupation for decades, if not centuries, undisturbed by predators other than humans. David felt that he should resent the intrusion, but on reflection he reasoned that they were only small, he was temporary, they would not try to talk to him, and they could all happily coexist. It was humans he was wanting to avoid after all, and he had the satisfying conviction that at least there were none present.

The agent had warned about many other things, in some puzzlement that anyone would be wanting a booking at this time of year, especially an extended one. Patiently explaining to the strange southerner that the weather could get a tad inclement up there. The place was usually locked up until spring, running on automatic timers. Communication may be difficult. He may not be able to leave when he wanted to. Better and better, the more that David heard. The right place, the right shape and the right time.

He had announced to any who would listen that he needed to get away for a while, to get in touch with his real values. He couldn't think of a better way to explain it, nor one that would be believed. Few people could see the point of going out to remotest nowhere simply to find what you had brought with you in the first place. Why not just shut himself inside at home, alone? Self-isolating. Plenty of values there. In any case, what is the point of values if there is no-one to share them with? What was he going to do when he found them? Were they even lost? So the questions went, an ineffectual pattering on a mind long resolved. They all meant well, but escape was what he needed.

There is a powerful attraction to an empty and isolated facility, fully equipped for the summer trade but left to its own devices until then. Something of value must surely lurk within, well worth a visit of a dark night when only the unwise or insane would venture near. Crowbars advised, knapsacks otherwise empty, awaiting reward. It is the way of the world, an integral part of its diverse values. A silent entry was preferable, just in case there really was an occupant. Expert leverage was duly being applied to an aging window frame that was perhaps more frail than the would-be intruders realised.

David was still drifting in patient contemplation. We enter this world alone, he reflected, and we most certainly leave it alone. Even in-between we live alone inside ourselves, thinking a billion thoughts that will never find expression. The longer we live, the more we know, and the less it helps us. David knew that not all of these reflections applied to him – but they fitted the story he told the world.

He remembered so many things about her, but he was starting to need a photograph to remember her face. So many years together, so many of them spent alone, walled in by the fear of communicating too much. He had lied, of course, about many things, but the entire truth would never have helped. Some secrets are best kept. She had been worth every day of it though, so he had stayed until her time in this world was done. There was only joy, and nothing to regret, not even his eventual solitude. All things pass, and the subtle glow of the ring on his finger hinted that his time here was also reaching its end, as time always does.

Whisky and music help to fuel such reverie, but seldom help to find meaningful conclusions. As he twisted the ring, his thoughts were abruptly interrupted by a dull thud from the room next-door, followed by the splintering sound of shattered glass. It jarred unpleasantly against the background of stringed instruments. It did not fit the mood.

The moment was ruined. David put down the whisky glass and grumbled. Did I leave a window open, surely not – I don't remember opening one. He rose resentfully to his feet to investigate. The agent had stressed that he would be responsible for upkeep during his stay, and he felt that he should honour the request.

The window frame in the back room was missing, most of it lying on the floor, surrounded by broken glass, some of which had scattered around the room. David stooped to pick up a nasty-looking fragment, still attached on one side to part of the window frame. As he rose, he found himself staring at a young man who had just pushed himself through what was now a yawning gap in the wall. A second face was looking through behind him.

"Shit, there really is somebody here!" The young man teetered between fight and flight, crowbar in hand, and appeared to come down in favour of the former, given the apparent odds. He addressed David. "Relax Grandpa, no need for anyone to get hurt." The second man was climbing through the breach, his eyes also on David.

David fingered the pane of glass in his hand, assessing the damage it could cause, briefly considering pointless violence. This was something he could most decidedly do without, time was short, but he could feel his old abilities sharpening in response to the unmistakeable signals from above. His world was balanced on the brink of change. A strange calm washed over him.

"I think you should leave gentlemen. It is important that I am alone right now. It is not safe for you here."

"Just relax pal!" The voice was anything but relaxed. "Drop the glass and turn around with your hands behind ya. This don't need to take long!"

David's anger was building, his true form almost showing. This was not what he had come here for and there was not time to explain. Almost too late, he remembered the wisdom of restraint. He shrugged his shoulders and dropped the glass, which fragmented further on the floor around his feet. Weaponry was not relevant.

The larger of the two men smiled, and they began to move towards him. Long forgotten instinct took over. He moved abruptly and raised one arm, as the years fell away from him. A flash of violet light from his ring, and the moment froze. The two men were locked motionless in the centre of the room, their faces fixed with expressions of fear and confusion.

Reassembling the moment was more difficult that he remembered from his apprenticeship. Transporting the two prone figures back out to the slippery causeway was straightforward, he hoped they would not remember. Restoring the former state of the shattered windowpanes proved more difficult – he made something of a mess of it. He felt a pang of guilt about that, but there was nothing more to be done in the borrowed time available.

The light in the tower continued to wink out its message. High above in the turbulent sky there was an answering wink from a familiar hulk, and he moved hurriedly back to the focal zone just as the music restarted. David's time had come at last. He was going home.

32 Ben and the Pen of the Worlds – Anila Syed

Withered hands trembled as they undid the paper.

"Here it is!" His pale blue eyes peered out from his wrinkled face like stars caught up in the net of time.

The box was old and coming apart, but he carefully removed the lid, almost reverentially, as if it was still in one piece.

Inside was just an old plastic fountain pen.

"Have you ever used it?" Ben asked, not able to tear his eyes away.

"Of course not." He sounded affronted at such a ridiculous question. "What would I write? What would I want?"

The old man considered for a second, his eyes leaving the room as his thoughts travelled to the distant past. He shook his head and a laugh escaped from his lips.

"Actually, so much. I wanted it all." But then he gestured around the opulent room; the lavish surroundings reflected their resident well.

"So you did use it?"

"I said, 'No', my boy." Suddenly he became alert. "There is power in the written word my lad," he said, sitting up. But it was too much activity. He sank back down into his chair just as rapidly.

"Didn't need to. I was lucky. In work, in love, in life." He laughed again, more strongly this time as he sank back into reverie.

Ben waited respectfully; the interview seemed to be over. After a few minutes, he switched his recorder off and slipped quietly away. The Pen of the Worlds tucked safely in his pocket.

* * * * * * * * * *

Ben had first heard about The Pen after a long, ridiculous night spent with a group of strangers he had hooked up with in the middle of the Caribbean. A girl had heard it straight from her friend that one of her acquaintances was the sister of the butler to a man who owned the Pen of the Worlds. A pen which would turn whatever you wrote into reality.

The butler was disgusted that this man, an elderly gentleman now in his nineties, had never even used the pen.

"He's always been too scared," the girl had said in a passable Irish accent, in what Ben had assumed must be an imitation of the butler.

What on earth is there to be scared of? Ben had asked, his thoughts fighting through a haze as his eyes blinked her into focus.

What indeed?

So here it was. An old blue plastic pen.

Ben picked it carefully out of his pocket and gingerly laid it onto a piece of paper on the table in front of him. In all his thirty two years, he had never been more... what?...disappointed by the sight of anything.

So what now?

"Well, pen," he said to it. "Let's test you out, shall we?"

He picked it up and dropped it almost at once, staring with a shocked expression. It had seemed to him that the pen had wriggled.

Stop being stupid.

He picked it up more firmly and quickly wrote, 'I want a Jaguar' on the paper in a bold hand.

After almost two minutes, Ben realised that he had not been breathing and, quickly gulping some air into his lungs, ran to the window to see whether there was anything parked outside.

[Time stood still. Between one blink and the next the familiar sun-dappled scene of the Amazon vanished to be replaced by a dark, grey pavement. The rotation of the earth was slowed for one microsecond as the new reality insinuated itself over the old.]

Ben sighed and sat back down in front of the paper. He picked up the pen. This time: 'I want a million pounds'. He hesitated then underneath he wrote, 'please'.

He looked around the room sheepishly.

['Shuuu-uck!' The tiny sounds of a million pounds sucking out of existence were heard by no-one in hundreds of bank vaults around the world. But the echoes along the corridors of time as the money failed to fulfil its destiny were silent.]

Ben was disgusted. This was worse than receiving a jigsaw puzzle at Christmas. Nothing had happened. No wonder the old fool claimed he had never used the pen. He had probably written hundreds of things but none of it had worked.

Maybe there was a code, or a ritual. He would have to do more research. Special ink perhaps?

Sluggishly, Ben wandered into the kitchen and switched the kettle on, then came back and did the same to the TV. It had taken him almost a year to track down the butler. Then it had taken almost all his savings to find out the identity of the old man and get to have an interview with him. There was no turning back now, he had too much time and effort invested in this.

The sound of the early evening news drifted in through the open door.

"And finally, a large cat has once again been seen roaming the streets of Sussex. Although reports of sightings do go back to the sixties and seventies, tonight, several Twitter users have reported seeing a large black puma-like animal. Police have cautioned the public not to approach anything they think is suspicious. Well, I don't know about you, but I'll be making sure to lock my doors and windows tonight. Goodnight."

But he was trying to figure things out. He was obviously asking for too much. Maybe if he had started small, then he had a better chance of getting what he wanted.

Let's see, something small. Getting no inspiration from the kitchen, he made his way back into the lounge and sat down. How about asking for some new trainers? That would be something small to ask for which would still come in useful.

'I would like some trainers.'

That was satisfactory. Ben sat back.

Even the sounds from the television could not fill the empty, expectant void which conspicuously, contained no trainers.

Maybe he should be more specific.

Underneath the words, he wrote 'now'. Then he added the date and time, just to be sure.

[The men had been on the way home. But for a reason which neither of them would ever remember, they turned right that evening and headed into town.]

Ben suddenly accepted the futility of it all. He was sitting alone in his room, writing pointless things on a piece of paper.

Someone must have played a great trick on him that night in the Caribbean. It was an elaborate hoax all right. Hadn't he ended up giving his money away to 'contacts' and informants?

Talking of hoaxes, there was some breaking news on TV. There were urgent red scroll bars racing along the bottom of the screen and the newsreader was looking especially cheerful: Something really horrible must have happened. Ben reached over for the remote and turned the volume up.

"Parts of central London have been disappearing. Police have set up diversions and are evacuating the residents of all central and South London areas. Terrorist activity is not suspected at this stage."

Then they cut to a reporter on location, but Ben hardly heard a word he said. The scene behind him was the most extraordinary chaos. It was as if pinpoints of reality had taken it upon themselves to float away. Parts of the view suddenly floated up for a short distance and then 'popped' out of existence.

A cold dread filled Ben's body like a shower of cold fireworks. Part of a car behind the reporter suddenly lifted up and headed off into space before vanishing.

The news reporter must have seen the look of shock in his cameraman's eyes because he took one look at the car and, shouting 'Let's get out of here,' ran off to the left. The cameraman turned tail and followed him, the image bobbing up and down as he ran.

Ben sat back and pushed his floppy brown hair back out of his eyes. He was not quite in central London, but it was near enough to worry. What if this was it? What if someone had left off some weird weapon that would mean the end of reality as we know it?

His mind whirred and his eyes fell on the pen. The Pen of the Worlds.

Well if this was it, then he was going to ask the pen for the big one, just in case.

With shaky fingers, he started to write:

'Lily, I loved you from the first moment I saw you. You had a coffee stain on your dress and a wonky smile and when you tripped over my bag, it was fate.

I'm sorry I am such a dope. I'm selfish and mean. I couldn't see that you were the best thing that ever happened to me and I let you go.

I let you walk out of that door and I have regretted it every single day since you left.

I want Lily Evans to love me again'. He took a deep breath.

Well, even if it did not work, he had voiced the one thing he wanted most in the world. The one thing which, if this was the end of existence, would make his life real again.

[Neurons realigned their synapses. Pathways of memory which had been forgotten for two long, agonising years, raw from the constant recriminations and scrutiny now resurfaced, clean and burnished. Tears fell.]

The sound of the phone crushed the silence.

"Hello?"

"...Ben."

"Lily?"

"I... I don't know why I wanted to phone you."

"Lily?!"

A slow smile started to work its way around Ben's mouth.

"It's so great to hear from you. It's been years. Er, how have you been?"

"Ben, I'm married."

"Oh."

"I'm calling from Tokyo actually."

"Er."

"Yes, I got a job out here, after we, after I left England. But something this morning – Ben, It's five o'clock in the morning here." She laughed softly.

[Reality unwound.]

"It's funny," Ben said adding airly. "I was just thinking about you." He turned the paper over as if Lily would see it down the phone line and find him out.

[The 'sense' was pushed out of the world. The course it had carved for itself was meaningless now. What was it going to do with the extra requirements? How would it cope? A building in Germany gave up and floated off into the ether.]

"We did have some great times," she laughed again.

They felt themselves drawing closer over the miles.

[The only way to cope with this problem was to rub it out and start again.]

"Ben?"

"Yes, I'm still here."

"Ben, something's happening. I feel sick." There was a scream.

Ben put a hand to his mouth. Then, "Lily? Lily are you there?"

"I'm disappearing. The room is vanishing. Help!"

Ben sat listening in shocked silence. What could he do?

His eyes swivelled to the TV. The news was on again and now the floating objects were bigger. Large chunks of London were escaping. The picture cut to Oslo, New Delhi, South Africa, it was the same all over the world.

"There is power in the written word, my lad." The words echoed in his brain.

Suddenly, explosively a corner of the lounge erupted. A gaping hole let Ben see into the street outside. But even there, existence was having a tough time holding on. It was being replaced by a grey nothing. As he looked down, horrified, the ground beneath him was beginning to disappear.

In no time at all, he found himself floating, the room dissolving. Sparks flew out of the TV and it shattered into huge fragments which came hurtling towards him.

A rough wind started to whistle around his ears as the firmament gave way to void.

This was it.

This was why the old man had not used the pen. The Pen was mightier than the world itself.

Words could create and they could destroy. And he, Ben had destroyed. He had been selfish and mean and he had thought of nothing but his own happiness. As consciousness started to drift away, he found that he was once more holding the pen.

With his last ounce of strength, he lifted his failing arm and wrote onto the grey which now surrounded him. There was only one word which filled his mind.

'STOP!'

33 The Pinging Cat – Robert Greener

Chapter 1 of 'Falling in Parallel'

*Most things that happen are not witnessed.
No sentient being perceives them, still less
records an account. Events leave their mark
around them, creating reality as they go. On
very rare occasions a distant echo may
eventually come to the attention of something
self-aware, provided it is not preoccupied
with matters of lesser importance...*

Something was not quite right about the hedge.
If the two witnesses looked closely, some of the
leaves seemed to flicker and flit in and out of
sight, or even existence, and a piece of the wall at
the end seemed to join in the fun, shimmering
ever so slightly in the pale spring sunshine.

A small furry creature with four legs was
moving along the line of the hedge. It had
greenish-grey colouring with a pattern of darker
stripes. At one end of its body was a tail, held up
in the air, as if to receive signals from afar. At the
other end was a head, topped by a pair of alert
and pointed ears, one of which looked a bit
damaged. There was a suggestion of sharp teeth
concealed within, and a languid predatory grace
to its movements.

The creature was intrigued by the subtle
oddity of the hedge as it interrupted its patrol
around what it regarded as the perimeter of its
territory – which was contested with other
creatures in the vicinity. Under normal

circumstances, one of the creature's tasks was to ensure that they all knew that it owned this space. Other creatures (for there were many) often failed to understand this point and it had spent a busy but successful night improving their grasp of territorial etiquette. The creature was no longer preoccupied by that concern, although it did stop to clean its damaged ear. It was not given to musing pointlessly about the past. The strange shimmering of the hedge belonged firmly to the present however.

The creature was distracted by a distinct rustling sound in the leaves of the hedge, close to where it met the wall. Its neural wiring, an influential pattern of connections housed within its head, advised it to investigate. The wiring was reporting the possible presence of an even smaller furry creature, which was likely to be edible, although hunger was not the reason for its interest. It had recently eaten in a nearby dwelling, which it partially shared with a different but related species of creature.

These other creatures differed in a number of important ways. For example, they were a great deal larger, and they moved about on two legs, rather than four. Another peculiarity was that they gave things names. Their name for themselves was 'human.' They also had a very short name for his species. They referred to him as a 'cat.' Some of them had a slightly longer and more specific name for him in particular, 'Sirius.' He was blissfully unaware that either of these names applied to him, although he did associate the sibilant sound with kindness or food.

These humans were very friendly to him, most of the time – it had been they who had installed the useful little door that opened when he approached. It was his portal to warmth and comfort. They had also placed a collar around his neck, a continuing source of annoyance to him. Despite this indignity, he even slept there most days, it was warm and dry, and he allowed some of the humans to sit warmly beneath him sometimes, provided they kept still. He was mostly content with life, although he was not aware of this. He just thought the world was like that.

Sirius did not know that he was unusual. He was, for example, particularly talented with regard to spatial awareness – even more so than most of his species. He tended to know what was around him and how to reach it. He was of course unaware of many other things, the majority of which were of no immediate importance to his existence. A good example would be the large tunnel that passed underneath the hedge some distance below the place where he was prowling. This tunnel bristled with some of the best technology available on this particular planet, with the sole practical purpose of causing very high-speed collisions between exceedingly small objects, if indeed that is what they were. This was in the hope of measuring what happened to the debris and finding out a little bit more about where they came from, whether or why they existed and what they might be made out of, if anything. Although the tunnel was currently active beneath his four feet, these matters were not his priority.

He was unaware that there was a human watching both him and the hedge, from an upstairs window, which was something that would have seemed important to him had he known. This human knew a lot about the tunnel underneath them and what it was for. For the human, it was one of the things that he thought was important and interesting – one of the defining interests of his life in fact. He spent a lot of time there. His specific name for himself was 'Andersen,' and he was what was known amongst humans as a 'scientist.'

Humans are also partially self-aware, in some ways similar to cats, but their awareness applies to different aspects of their existence. Unlike cats, some of these things cause them to worry a lot, because they have an uncomfortable relationship with the present tense. They prefer to think and fret about what has happened in the past and even more so about what might happen in the future.

They are lost in time.

Although Sirius knew very little about the many things that happen inside the heads of humans, he did know that they exhibited some very odd behaviours. This human was brushing his teeth, as the cat had sometimes seen humans doing, along with other strange habits, like intentionally standing under a stream of hot water. He vaguely understood that many of them worry about the condition of their teeth, despite tolerating other imperfections. The cat may have wondered why they bother with their dirty and mostly useless ears, which barely seemed to hear anything, or their strangely shaped noses, that largely failed to smell anything. Human teeth seemed important to them, but they did not look very impressive to Sirius, who had a much sharper set. Humans seemed to him like an oversized version of something he might otherwise try to eat.

* * * * * * * * * *

Andersen was watching the scene below with evident interest. He admired cats, the graceful way they moved, their unworried detachment from the norms of social expectations that frequently paralysed him. Those who knew him often joked that he should have been born as a cat, he seemed to have a special affinity with them – a particular kind of curiosity, the need to investigate, and a tendency to follow his own path.

On this occasion, his attention was focussed not on the cat, but on the subtle disappearing dance of the leaves, and the almost imperceptible hint of strange light glimmering somewhere around them. He thought it looked interesting – exactly the kind of shape-shifting that leaves normally don't do. He was pondering that, the sort of thing he did a lot.

His eye was drawn to the cat, who was crouching, waggling its rear end and twitching its tail, seemingly stalking something nearby. Andersen could not see what it might be. Everything went still, apart from the cat's tail, twitching about with a mind of its own. A leaf stirred in an odd way; the cat leapt in an even odder way, as if changing course at the last moment…

And disappeared.

It unpeeled itself from existence, fragmenting in mid-air, with a strange squeaky high-pitched plop, almost a ping, as it slid away into nowhere!

Andersen blinked in surprise and spilt a bit of foaming toothpaste down his chin. Even his useless human ears had heard the high-pitched noise. He continued to stare at the spot, which still seemed to shimmer gently. A few moments later, the shimmering dissipated, and the hedge ceased its flickering dance, offering nothing further by way of explanation.

As he continued to watch the perplexing scene, there was a movement near the wall of the next-door house, not far away. The face of what might have been a cat seemed to emerge out of thin air, but not in a good way – bones and pink flesh were showing, around a row of exposed teeth, almost as if its head had been turned inside-out – but with no obvious sign of distress. As Andersen stared at this new apparition, the grisly face twisted about, briefly shape-shifting itself into something more cat-like before reversing the process – unpeeling itself once more and disappearing.

Andersen shook his head in confusion, but the scene did not change again. Deep in his soul, he knew that hedges do not eat cats – and he did not have the impression that the cat was injured, despite its appearance. The event was firmly logged in the category he reserved for the inexplicable, deserving of the closest attention and analysis. Nothing happens without cause, and although none came immediately to mind, the wheels had begun to turn in the back of his consciousness, searching for connections.

Still shaking his head, the train of his thoughts was derailed by the unwelcome realisation that he was supposed to be preparing to be somewhere else, a place referred to as 'work.' He turned and walked away from his bedroom window, back to the bathroom, where there were sounds from someone taking a shower. He needed to wipe his chin and get rid of the toothpaste before he could probe any more mysteries. "The weirdest thing!" he exclaimed to his reflection in the mirror, once he had succeeded.

There was a reaction from behind him, "The weirdest what?"

"A cat! It suddenly disappeared. Into thin air! And there was a sound. Quite loud. A kind of ping."

"I did hear something. Didn't sound like a cat though. More like a phone getting a text. I thought it was yours."

Andersen reflected for a moment and tried again. "There was a cat outside. It disappeared when I was looking right at it. Very odd indeed... I think it must belong to the next-door neighbour."

The sounds of the shower continued, but now there was a slightly thoughtful silence hiding within it.

"You mean Oliver? I don't understand. I don't think he has one, and cats don't make noises like that... Cats are quite good at disappearing, aren't they?"

"It twisted towards the wall and disappeared into thin air" continued Andersen, thinking aloud. "Must be a cat door there I didn't see. Or something... Looked out afterwards, somehow – it looked wrong – then went back in again."

"But cat doors don't make noises like that either! They just flap."

"Perhaps it has a magnetic mechanism that opens for the cat. With a noise, like a doorbell, so people know the cat has arrived..." Andersen trailed off; this was not a workable theory for what he had seen. "Or maybe a rusty hinge. Very rusty..." This didn't work either.

The sound of water from the shower slowed and stopped. A more playful voice now, "Well, maybe you could ask about it."

"Ask who?" said Andersen, whose mind was wandering in search of something that seemed like it might be important.

"The next-door neighbour Andersen! Oliver! Maybe he will even introduce you to the cat!"

"Yes, yes, maybe." Andersen had not really been listening. "I think I should go down and have a look first though. Very odd..."

Andersen's partner Arabella emerged from the shower and reached for a towel with an amused look on her face. She was a tall and striking woman in her early thirties with long light-brown hair and blue-grey eyes, a combination that had fascinated Andersen ever since they had met at University, almost a decade previously.

"You're a very strange man, but you are often right. Experimental evidence is needed, yes? Direct observation?" She was smiling, but there was a hint of irritation in her eyes.

Andersen was indeed an unusual man, in that he had a good eye for unexplained events and how to go about explaining them – it was how he spent a lot of his time and earned his living. He was also thought to be easily distracted, and Arabella's lack of clothing had momentarily crowded out the business of the cat in his partial awareness. For a human, Andersen was reasonably good at focussing on the present. The pursuit of mysteries receded into his subconscious, but did not disappear.

Andersen appeared to forget about a lot of things. He preferred to immerse himself in the moment, following the lines of his curiosity. This contributed to his considerable investigative abilities, but could be a source of mild frustration to some of his friends and colleagues. It is true that Arabella, clothed or otherwise, had a distracting effect on a lot of people. Moments could have a lot going for them if you went with the flow.

He was about three years older than she was, with a reasonably athletic build but a slight tendency to weight gain that he occasionally made efforts to resist. He had an open and friendly face with soft brown eyes that made a lot of people around him feel relaxed. He didn't know this; he just thought the world was like that.

There was however an indefinable strangeness about him that affected some people after a while. No-one could quite put their finger on it, but there were people who tried to avoid him for reasons they would not have been able to explain. Andersen didn't know this either, despite Arabella's best efforts to describe it. She said she loved his intelligence and occasional wisdom, but always felt both relaxed and uneasy at the same time in his presence. It was one of the things that she said made him interesting, even if she could not say why, and she liked people who were interesting.

"Can I have a bit of space please, I need to dry myself." She smiled, "You'll be late for work!"

Andersen had still been staring. He withdrew as requested into the bedroom, and found himself looking at an old small-framed photograph on the back of a dressing table. It showed the two of them at an outdoor party, fresh faced and beautiful, as young people so often are, without realising it. It was the day they had met; one of her friends had taken it. Andersen always thought that it revealed his shy awkwardness in contrast to Arabella's photogenic and self-assured presence – although he did remember that while he hadn't quite known what to say to her in his thunderstruck state, she didn't seem to want to mingle with anyone else either.

He reflected that before he met Arabella, his approaches to women had for years been characterised by a certain inbuilt pessimism, beginning from the assumption that anyone he fancied was likely to be out of his league. This partly stemmed from the subject he was obsessively studying. Announcing yourself as a theoretical physicist tended to be something of a conversation killer at the average party. Almost too late he had grasped the reality that she liked him, and was nonplussed by his apparent indifference. She had been his bedrock ever since, a natural source of stability and structure that he knew he sorely needed, even if he forgot it from time to time. And she was right that he would be late for work if he didn't get going.

Andersen looked up as his mind snapped back to the strange event he had just witnessed. He knew enough about cats to be aware that cat doors don't need doorbells. That is the whole point of a cat door – to let cats come and go without disturbing anyone. Cats wouldn't use one that made a pinging noise anyway, it just isn't dignified, and they hate being undignified. Andersen knew all of this. He had recovered himself, his curiosity had returned, and he was heading down to investigate the mystery of the shimmering hedge. Arabella was right; he needed data...

34 The Stop of Alessa Cassalva – Anila Syed

Light played on the surface of the water – a dappled melody of two interfaces, bringing out the best in each other. Anticipation filled Alessa's thoughts. If Merin was water, did that mean she was the light? She swam in the way he had shown her: head down, snorkel positioned high up and arms loose at her sides. She kicked back strongly with her legs. The water was energising as it eddied around her; she would soon be at the promontory.

Merin was waiting in the water today. He looked up as he saw her approaching. Alessa caught her breath as she sighted his tanned arms. His brown hair gleamed in the sunshine. She thought about his keen brown eyes and the way he smiled through his frown when he was focussing on something. Concentrate, she thought. Mustn't drown!

The merman was unlike anyone Alessa had known before. 'Such a cliché!' she had laughed to her friends. But it was true. For one thing, his emotions wore no guard. It was confusing and gave her some of the most startling and exhilarating days she had ever experienced. Startling because she was a human? Maybe she was just a scared little sea creature after all – hiding.

"I made you a thing," he said.

"A thing?"

"A... a... gift?"

He swirled his hands around and the surface of the sea began to spin. His hands were so inghle-vlin – a word he had taught her – attractive, irresistible, enticing, compelling. Strong feelings crammed into three syllables.

'It is what I feel for you,' he had said. 'In here.' He thumped his chest, sending some of the shells that clung to his body flying off.

How could she resist that? She felt herself move towards him when he said it, just wanting to be close to him. And never leave?

The spinning water rose, glowing grey with the reflected colours of his tail and her human skin swirling in the droplets. Two heart shapes began to appear, intertwined, revolving around each other. He held it for a few moments before letting it sink back under the surface.

"That was beautiful!" Alessa said.

He lifted her out of the water easily and spun her round.

"It is this," he said, pulling her near.

Alessa draped her lithe brown arms around his neck and nestled herself into his warm body. She could feel her heart revolving around his. Getting too close. They kissed.

* * * * * * * * * *

Alessa woke with a jolt. She ripped off the snorkel, which returned to a VR visor in her hands. The beach and the lovely palm trees melted away and became her living room once again.

She looked down at her hand. No longer limber as it was in her avatar, her real skin was lined and loose. Only a few more days until the Stop.

Procrastination would not help her to write her Speak, even if it was such glorious procrastination. How did she love Merin so much? How had he made her a gift? That wasn't supposed to happen.

Her Stop was scheduled exactly on her 50th rotation. Her doctor, Logan, had said that her cells might still be functioning optimally for a few more years, but had decided on the exact day for neatness. She sat down to write the final words that she wanted to say to the world.

* * * * * * * * * *

Alessa was lying on the beach and Merin was combing her hair.

"Merin?"

"Yes?"

"What would you say if it was the last thing you were ever going to say?"

Merin leaned over and looked down at her face upside-down.

"What? What do you mean, 'the last thing'"?

"Just that – if it was your last day and you had to say your last words?"

Merin's brows furrowed: "Alessa, are you going somewhere?"

This threw her. In all the preparation, all the social events, the invitations, Alessa had not thought to tell him about the Stop. Why would she?

"Erm...," she said. How could she have this conversation with this ... with him?

"I'm kind of finish...shing." She hunted for the right words. "Everything."

Merin looked like he was going to be sick.

"You're going to stop coming here? I will not be able to live without you, Alessa, my inghle-vlin."

"Merin, you know...," she paused. You know you're not real, right?

Alessa thought about the constant, creative gifts he gave her, the words he taught her and the way he made her feel.

"Alessa, I love you!"

"Merin, you don't! How can you?" Panic was rising in her chest. Was her merman paradise game starting to turn sour? Why did this moment feel so real?

"Less, ever since I met you, you have awoken a tokna inside me – a...a... feeling. I can't describe it."

"No!"

Alessa ripped her snorkel off her face and flung the visor away but then gasped as she saw what was in the room: The image of two swirling hearts floated in the air before her. She crumpled to the floor, sobbing as if her world was being torn apart.

* * * * * * * * * *

Three thousand people in her section were Stopping this cycle. The hall was packed and buzzing. In the upper galleries, spectators filled the ranks, busy with the chatter of expectation.

Stoppers wore yellow clothes during the last few stages, gradually progressing to bright red on the final day. The lower seats were vibrant with hues from sunflower to ochre to gold.

Alessa fought her excitement, trying hard to tamp down the butterfly bubbles rising up from her stomach.

"This will be your pinnacle moment!" Logan cried from somewhere behind the stage.

"We have grown to be our BEST! We will shine brighter than the REST! We will STOP!" The entire crowd shouted as one and then erupted into wild cheering as Logan appeared before them.

Logan was elegant and tall with swept back, blond hair.

"Stoppers!" he yelled. "You'll be watching your process videos today. After the commitment ceremonies next month, you will all be making your pledges and saying your Speaks. Are you ready to STOP?"

"Ready!"

Alessa hesitated. She had been completely ready – in her heart and mind – but now? She

177

could not rid herself of thoughts of Merin. Every few minutes, in her mind, she saw glimpses of his eyes, his smile, or his hands – his inghle-vin hands – the sun on his hair, the way he smelled of the warm, fresh sea.

Underneath the elation of completing her life, Alessa felt a heavy weight in her chest. It was terrible to admit it: she didn't want to leave him.

"Now then," Logan was saying. "Does anyone have any questions?"

* * * * * * * * * *

"Dr Logan?" Alessa found him after the ceremony.

"Alessa!" he cried. "Are you ready to Stop?"

"Dr Logan, I wanted to ask you..." She lowered her gaze.

"Of course! Fire away!"

"I wanted to ask you what happens if we don't want to Stop?"

Logan looked as if he had been struck by lightning.

"If you don't...?"

"Yes, if you don't want to? What happens?"

"Alessa, all the tests are in. Your Stop is scheduled. I mean, you haven't signed your commitment yet, but that's just a formality really. Have you changed your mind? I mean, it's all settled!" His energy fizzled away. He looked totally exasperated.

Alessa closed her eyes. An image of Merin diving into the water crossed her mind. She shook her head but couldn't stop the feeling of longing in her heart that turned into a shudder.

"I just wondered if I could, you know, stay a bit longer?" she said sheepishly.

"Now come on, what's all this about? I mean, don't you want to die at the top of your life? Do you think you should go on and let your cells go past their optimal condition?" He looked at her quizzically, as if he had won an argument.

"No! Of course not! But, well, I...," she trailed off.

"It would be doing a grave injustice to yourself, to your family, to the planet. Is that what you want?"

"No, of course not!"

* * * * * * * * * *

Merin found her sobbing on the beach.

"Alessa, what's wrong?"

She lifted a tear-stained face to his.

"Merin, I'm going to go away. I have to give a speech to tell everyone about my life achievements and then I will be gone forever, but all I can think of is you," she broke down again. He kissed her face, her tears, her eyes.

"Lessa, isn't that good? Why don't you tell them all about me? About us?"

"What? Oh, but I couldn't!"

"Yes, why don't you tell them about our lives here and about how we love each other? Maybe they would let you stay?"

Alessa considered this as she switched out of the game.

Let her stay?

That night, Alessa dreamt that Merin was in her room with her, in her bed.

* * * * * * * * * *

The training was a torture of agony. While the other participants whooped and cheered through the videos and their commitments, Alessa had been drawn and wan. Merin. Her every breath was Merin, every step, every thought: Merin's arms, Merin's back, Merin's shoulders, Merin's beautiful, beautiful tail. She felt his lips on her neck, his hands on her back. Breathing was difficult, focus was impossible.

How could she get out of this?

But today was her Speak and tomorrow was…her resolve collapsed inside… tomorrow was her Stop.

Logan was brushing back his hair with his fingers.

"Thank you, Reeba, that was enchanting.

"Next, can we have Alessa on the stage." He turned to face her with a rigid stare as she walked onto the stage and up to the podium. The cameras of the world were turned upon her.

In the past few weeks, Logan had spent many minutes chatting with her and knew about her whole situation. This puppy-love infatuation that she had developed with a character in a computer game. He had sent her to a psychologist to bring her to her senses and see that if she missed this chance, she would turn older, her cells would start to misfunction – then who knows what would happen? They showed her ancient videos of the times before, when diseases of old age meant that billions of pounds were spent caring for old people; looking after sick people; paying old people to still be alive. What kind of world had that been with all that sickness and disease everywhere? Old people using up valuable resources long past the time that they were useful to society. The ugliness of old age had been wiped out by the compassion and caring that was represented by the Stop.

Alessa adjusted the microphone and stared out over the audience of red-clad Stoppers and their families seated in the upper galleries. Reeba's speech had been exultant and the crowd were in a jubilant mood. Someone whooped.

She gulped.

"H-hello everybody. My name is Alessa Cassalva, and I am 50 years rotated today."

The audience broke into wild applause.

Alessa looked down at her papers. She had written a lovely Speak about her work and her life.

She looked over at Logan. He smiled encouragingly then nodded towards the crowd.

"I wanted to speak to you today about my life's work. I am a reality engineer."

More applause from the crowd.

"For the past 6 years, I have been developing a game, Bliss," she gulped. "Many of you know of it, I think. Bliss lets you completely lose yourself. Had a difficult day? Visit the shores of Bliss. Feeling a little low? Let Bliss take away your cares.

"But what you don't know is that the game has come alive. Bliss is real, the game, the place. It's all real. And there is someone who lives in the game." She paused and pressed the button to start her slideshow. A picture of Merin appeared on the giant screen above her head. She heard someone in the audience gasp.

"And I am worried about what will happen." She turned to look at the screen. "I can not bear to think that he might no longer exist when I am gone.

"Merin!" she said, loudly. "Please let all assembled know that you are here and that you are real."

The picture of Merin started moving. The waves rolled, a breeze blew through the palm trees and Merin himself, blinked and waved through the screen. He had worn a shell necklace around his neck and he had adorned his hair with a red rhododendron flower for this occasion.

"I am Merin," he said. "Alessa is my love."

He seemed to be looking out over the audience.

"I know some of you will know love. Some of you will know what it feels like to be away from your loved ones, know the pain I feel when she leaves me, but please–" His image seemed to be turning to look at Logan. "Please, don't take my Lessa away from me forever. My only wish is that we can be together."

Merin turned to Alessa.

"Lessa, please," he begged. "Please don't leave me."

There was silence in the hall and mutters from the crowds.

Alessa turned nervously to Logan.

Logan came up to the podium. He covered up the microphone.

"Look, Alessa, I thought you were ready," he whispered. "Don't let this...this game take your chance at your glorious moment."

He turned to face the crowd: "Please give a round of applause for this amazing demonstration of Alessa's life! Thank you, Alessa, you may be seated."

On the screen above them, Merin roared.

"No!" he yelled.

"I can't let you take her forever! I am not a game!" he shouted.

He pointed at Alessa and lightning blazed from his fingers.

The lightning hit its mark; Alessa vanished.

* * * * * * * * * *

Months later, Logan's phone buzzed. There was a message.

He frowned at the text:

"We are Bliss, an immersive reality game spreading like wildfire across the worlds. We have perfect beaches, flawless sunsets and a family of Merpeople. Please know that Bliss is recognised as a world of sentients, created by its founders, the merman, Merin and the human, Alessa Cassalva. We invite all those who don't wish to Stop, to stop by!"

Spiritual and Esoteric

35 Guided meditation for Writing Group – Briar Noonan

It is early morning after what turned out to be a sleepless night, desperately searching for inspiration for your new writing project. You tried everything to get off to sleep, reading a book first of all, that usually works, especially the soporific tome you are currently forcing yourself to finish, but when even that failed to summon Morpheus you gave in and threw back the covers to slouch into the kitchen for a hot, milky drink. Sure to do the trick, that and the resolution to not even try to pummel your recalcitrant brain into submission, just let it go, snuggle down, think of nothing, just let go. Actually, trying to think of nothing is the worst thing you could have chosen to do, it is almost impossible!

As dawn starts to light up your bedroom window, you finally admit defeat and decide to go out into what promises to be a glorious day. Throwing on last nights' cast-off clothes and promising yourself a shower after you have worked up a sweat by doing at least ten thousand steps, you walk into the kitchen, grab your backpack lying on the tiles by the door and stuff into it the bare essentials that you never leave the house without. A bottle of water, a few granary bars, one of then covered in chocolate, your new virgin notebook that is just waiting to be filled with magnificent prose and your trusty pen, re-filled and ready to go.

Stepping out into the mild spring day the next question if where to go? Everywhere around home is so familiar, looking around you can see the same old roads, the same old houses, the same old characters bustling or bumbling along. Apart from...... that strange bunch of trees across the road, surely you would have seen them before, their slim barks covered in silver and their pale green, narrow leaves trembling in the warm air? You move off to investigate and approaching the stand of silver birch trees you discover that they are actually on a lip of raised ground, their shallow newly formed roots clinging onto the moist leaf mulch, but exposed to sight on the other side of the mound of earth as it falls away into the deep forest stretching into the distance. The smell of last year's damp leaves is intoxicating as the aroma reaches your nostrils from the trammelled earth beneath your boots. Adventure beckons and you step off the edge of the world you know and into the unknown forest.

There is a path of sorts, leading under the out flung branches of the bigger trees on either side as you penetrate deeper into the forest. The air is redolent with that 'green' smell that permeates your whole being and slowly the heavy fug that is the aftermath of your sleepless night, starts to dissipate. How can you be dispassionate about the cheerful birdcalls which now envelop you, drawing you in with their sheer zest for life, their eager embrace of the spring that is now in bud.

Having lost all sense of direction and purpose in such arboreal meanderings it comes as a pleasant surprise to find yourself entering a woodland glade, empty apart from one huge tree standing alone in the centre. It towers over the clearing, its foliage newly minted and in shades of bright, glossy green against the smooth light brown trunk and branches. Dimly, in the distance, you can just hear the sound of tinkling laughter and note the traces of footprints in the soft grass lying at the base of the tree, sculptured in the hollows between its mighty roots forming soft, inviting bowers which still bear the impression of human forms amongst the bent stems. Above such a one you can see that there is a carving newly dug into the smooth bark, a heart and two sets of initials pierced by a carefully drawn arrow. This is obviously a trysting place for lovers for there are many other hearts carved upon the tree, many so old that it is difficult to decipher the letters.

Finding the glade empty and the soft grass inviting you decide to stop and refresh yourself by sitting against the bole of the tree and opening your bag of supplies, taking out the water and snack bar. Perhaps this spot will provide the inspiration that you have been lacking for far too long? Tenderly running a thumb across the soft leather binding on your notebook, you flirt with the possibility of drawing that out of the bag too, and settling back comfortably you consider the possibility of writing a love story. The very ground that you sit upon holds memories of lovers' meetings and surely the wise old body that you lean against could tell a story if only it had a tongue. Slowly the images start to come into your head, the possible story lines of young lovers meeting here to make their promises to each other only to break them as new loves come along. Sweethearts saying their goodbyes as life's circumstances contrive to tear them apart. The potential is endless, the scenarios so convoluted that the inspiration becomes self-defeating as you pick up your book to make a start, however, that first elusive sentence is not ripe for writing yet, so with a sense of defeat you rest your weary head back against the trunk which supports your shoulders.

Slowly, so slowly that you are not aware of it, the clamorous ideas chasing each other through your over-active brain disappear, leaving behind a silence never before experienced. Your thoughts become slow, ponderous, as the sound of the breeze soughing through the branches overhead gradually takes on the quality of a voice, murmuring softly yet insistently and difficult to ignore. It talks of times long past, when the forest was young and untrammelled by the passage of humans, lovers or otherwise. It speaks of the fall of the seed into the rich earth, of the cold winter whilst it lay dormant and the returning warmth of spring as it put out its slow shoots and roots. There were years upon years of subtle growth, of small creatures who made its branches their homes, as they mated and procreated and died to give place to others that came and went in the same endless repeating cycle.

The tree had seen many lovers, witnessed their coming together and their vows and promises, their joy and their broken hearts, the celebration of the love they shared, and later, witnessed with stoicism the carving of his skin to hold their memories. But still he did not understand love in the manner in which humans do, how could he? He is not driven by a power greater than himself to find a mate, he does not feel incomplete when he is singular for that is his natural state. Another tree encroaching upon his space would only take away the nutrients that his body needs, and other arms entwined with his own would take away the sun from his canopy of leaves, the leaves that feed him and drip the moisture to his thirsty roots. In due season he had flowered and alone had produced seeds as he felt the sap rise through his being, but all this he had done as part of his solitary life cycle, without mating in any way that makes him less, or more, than himself.

Imperceptibly, the impressions that you have experienced through your communion with this ancient being start to fade away but they have left behind them so many questions within your heart about the nature of love. Too many questions to allow you to put pen to paper at this time and so it is with a gentle hand upon the smooth bark of your recent confidant that you rise, gather your belongings once more into your backpack and make a slow exit from the glade.

The land slopes gently down towards the shimmer of water just glimpsed in the distance whilst high above the sun is reaching its zenith in a clear blue sky. There are white wisps of jet trails crossing the blank canvas provided by such a clear day and birds busily foraging in the hedgerows and bramble patches which abound on all sides.

The prospect of sitting by a lake seems like the perfect culmination of your walk and so, heading in the direction of that brief view of sunlit water, you continue along the gently meandering path.

It is not long before the trees and bushes thin out and allow you to see the perfect vista waiting at the end of the path. The lake is smooth, hardly touched by the breeze and reflects the blue of the sky above whilst all around the trees are reflected as in a mirror, slightly shimmering but true in colour and in almost every detail. Around the edges of the lake there are small rocks and pebbles lying on ground which is almost sandy, smooth and soft like the brown sugar Mum used to make cakes with. Strange how something so simple can evoke childhood memories of sitting in the kitchen on a high stool, impatiently waiting for the opportunity to scrape the bowl clean and naughtily, lick the spoon.

Putting down your bag and once again taking out the slightly warm bottle of water, the remembered indulgence of childhood leads you to choose the chocolate covered snack bar to accompany it as you sink down onto the soft ground. Thoughts return to the knotty question of a writing topic and the premise that, if it is at all possible to be inspired by nature, surely, you think, this is the day and the place for it. Strangely, the only idea which comes is for a crime novel, a vastly competitive genre and therefore, maybe just the challenge that you need. Turning over ideas in your head you toss a rounded stone from palm to palm, just playing with ideas.

There is a large black stone not too far away and you drag it into a clear space at the water's edge to represent 'the baddy' in your blossoming scenario. Male? Female? You have yet to decide. Obviously, your crime novel will need a main character, the hero or heroine and so you place a slightly smaller white stone on top of the black one where they lay quite still, opposites but in close proximity as they will be throughout your plot. There will need to be other characters, secondary ones but these should be nicely drawn and well rounded, so for each you choose another stone to represent them and place each on top of the balanced cairn that is being constructed, it is quite high now but it is becoming more difficult to maintain balance as the complexity of your internal narrative develops. In your mind's eye you can almost see the final twist, the exposure of the villain and the approbation of your hard-working main character as he/she achieves justice. The final stone to be placed on top must be perfect in colour and shape, but not too big nor too heavy or the scales of justice, your cairn, will be toppled. Spying the perfect capstone you move a pace to the water's edge, but, stooping to retrieve it you are distracted as you catch sight of your reflection in the pool and stop just for a moment, blindly placing the small stone behind you on top of the tall tower.

The image that distracted you for a moment, your own mirror image, has started to move, even though you are not doing so, it reaches out an arm towards you even though yours remain firmly by your side. Its eyes, your eyes, are entreating you to come, to come where? Into the water? This is absolute madness but under some strange sort of compulsion your feet seem to have developed a will of their own and are shuffling into the edge of the lake. Your feet should be feeling cold and wet, so should your legs because as you look down in surprise you see that the water now reaches up to your knees, but there is no sensation of coolness or moisture, not even discomfort as you continue to answer the beckoning that calls so undeniably.

Looking up from the deepening water you notice that the figure which is drawing you on is losing its mirror like image of you, now it is more of a disturbance in the clear water, as though the humanoid figure is composed of nothing more that currents of water within the greater stillness of the lake. As the water creeps up towards your neck and chin, common sense should firmly take over and make you abandon this foolishness, can you even swim? You are certainly not suicidal even if your creative faculties **are** on a break. Holding your breath, you accept the inevitable as your disobedient feet take you yet further under the water, which is still not evidenced by your sense of feeling, only by that of sight.

How long can you hold your breath for? Two minutes? five? Eventually desperation takes over and you cannot hold your breath any longer and it is with a feeling of impending doom and mindless desperation you draw in a breath, a perfectly normal breath, no choking, no water rushing in to fill up your lungs and drown you, no frantic panic as your life revue rushes before you in a last farewell to mortal existence. Strangely enough you feel absolutely normal, even invigorated as the beckoning figure leads you deeper into the depths.

Having abandoned caution to the winds and presuming that you are somehow in a lucid dream after collapsing with exhaustion on the sunny bank that is rapidly disappearing from view, you follow the swirling figure deeper into the lake. Glancing upwards to the surface of the water, which is now about two feet above your head you notice something floating there, something which seems vaguely familiar. Closer inspection reveals the object to be your precious, virgin, notebook, the anticipated receptacle of all your imagination and closely woven plot lines, its blank pages splayed open and waving gently in the water. You reach up a hand to pull it closer but to no avail, it is just that little bit too far out of reach.

Your surroundings are somehow becoming more solid and strangely familiar. Walls have formed around you that are the exact colour of the decor in your home, there is even a comfy couch there just to one side of an identical reproduction of your overburdened coffee table. With an overwhelming feeling of bemusement your legs weaken, and you sink down onto your favourite perch, your refuge from work and escape from the demands of daily life. As if by magic, for this is surely what is happening, your favourite drink appears on the table flanked by naughty but nice cream cakes, it would be such a shame not to eat them, they would only get soggy if left here uneaten and they are far too fattening for the fish.

Your nemesis is now sitting comfortably on the floor in front of the television set with its back....your back? towards you, watching your all-time favourite movie. Your entire surroundings confirm your diagnosis of this entire episode being a dream. It has obviously been proven by featuring all your favourite indulgences as the ultimate wish fulfilment dream should do. Indolence beckons as the notebook which is so far removed from your view overhead disappears from sight, and almost from memory. Almost, but not quite.

Is this a familiar experience? Are there too many temptations in life for you to really settle down to the hard slog of writing? Is it something which you put off for another day, promising yourself that when you have **just** had a cup of tea, or something stronger, when you have **just** finished that bit of housework or **just** cleared the decks from other more pressing matters, **then** you will get down to some serious writing.

The nebulous figure sitting with its back to you, absorbed in the movie is recognisable, once again as yourself as you acknowledge where you have come to in this emotional 'slough of despond,' to quote another great writer. How easy it is to stay here with all your little needs catered for, and how hard to overcome yourself. Standing and pushing away from the self that you have been shown, you search the waters above to find once more the glimpse of the elusive symbol of your intent, your notebook floating high above.

It matters not whether you can swim for this water is so obviously not real but merely a representation of your inner dynamic, the emotions which flood your being at times. Only the force of your will can propel you upwards towards your dreams. Only the strength of your own desire can overcome inertia, and only you

can pull yourself out of this situation.
Understanding that the only thing between you
and your creative output is your own weakness,
the self-knowledge causes you to gradually start
to rise higher in the water, leaving behind the too
comfortable nest that you have been wallowing in.
Feel the strength of your aspiration as it take you
closer to the object of your desires as you stretch
out a hand and clasp the notebook that
symbolises your ambition, fiercely to your breast.
The lesson of this place is that whatever you cast
into the waters will be returned to you as the tide
changes, and the resources that are your
emotions must be utilised well, not allowed to
swamp your will.

It comes as no great surprise to find that you
are lying beside the pool, notebook in one hand
and the other trailing the bottom of the cairn
which you had built earlier. Look at it. Did you
manage to place the final stone on top without
the whole edifice tumbling to the ground? Or is
the tower that you built so carefully strewn
around the water's edge because your judgement
failed to balance your plot well enough. Words
have power and your use of them must be finely
judged and balanced.

Taking up your bag you replace your book
safely within the pocket and head back into the
forest on the return journey home. It is up a
slight hill but thanks to the rest you have had the
gentle climb to the top does not take too long and
the final stretch through the woodland draws you
into the solace of its green shade.

The path is clearly defined and leads predictably to the glade where the huge sentinel of the forest waits for the next pair of lovers who should stray across this magical glade. Feeling as though you should make your farewells you draw closer to the huge tree, admiring its smooth bark which has inspired so much artistry with a penknife. There seems to be a new addition amongst all the hearts that decorate its span, just where you had been resting. The sap is still moist in the carven heart shape and it is easy to decipher the initials, for they are your own! Just yours, no others set underneath promising eternal love, even more intriguing is the carving that cuts through the heart, not an arrow as one would expect but a beautifully executed depiction of a pen!

It is but a short distance back to your own front door as you leave the forest behind, musing on what you have learnt. Musing, an appropriate word, for you do indeed feel as though you have met your own muse this day. The message of the freshly carved heart is directed solely at you and tells you without words that you must truly love yourself in order to stimulate your own creativity and banish the oft heard cry of "but I am not good enough!" But why is the heart pierced by a finely executed pen? Into your head comes the well-known phrase, "the pen is mightier than the sword" or indeed the arrow, for both can pierce just as surely, with cruelty or with desire.

The bank on which the new birch trees had stood is now level with the forest floor and the transition from earth to concrete beneath your feet is seamless. Entering your own room it is almost with a sense of déjà vue that your collapse onto your comfortable sofa, hot drink in hand, biscuits on the coffee table.

What you do next is in your own hands.

36 How it Began – Robert Greener

Neuroscience assures me that my earliest memory is vanishingly unlikely to be genuine. My fledgeling brain would not have been sufficiently formed. But I simply cannot imagine how it came to me if it is not real.

I remember being born. I was there. Me.

Perhaps I tell a lie. What I remember was the moment before being born. Specifically the tactile sensation. Squeezed, by a tight tube. Propelled through it at increasing speed, but no feeling of fear. I burst out into what I can only describe with language as a kaleidoscope of flashing light and colour and gibberish sounds, a fast-forward video. Nothing coherent. I was not aware of the passage of time – but a lot must have passed because the kaleidoscope resolved suddenly into a small me standing in a kitchen next to my mother. I do not know how old I was but I would guess between two and three years, maybe older. My mother was making something with what I now recognise as a Kenwood Chef. For some reason I walked outside, where something frightened me. I was later told that a scaffolding pole had fallen nearby – the kitchen was still being built, apparently.

Memory is an unreliable witness. It continually reforms in ways to fit in with how we want to perceive ourselves. Neuroscience has a lot to say about the storytelling abilities of our brains. Locked inside their bony prisons, they are constrained to build narratives to give coherence to the sensory inputs they receive from the outside world they imagine to exist.

This is a polite way of saying that we make up quite a lot of our memories. I do however believe that some truth remains.

This is what my neurons record. I had a flash of consciousness at the moment of my birth. It laid down a memory long before it is supposedly possible, then waited years before laying down another one.

But I have a deep conviction that I was conscious beforehand. There was communication somehow, I didn't feel alone. I don't know what that was.

But I was there. Me.

37 The Special One – Life spent in the quest of knowledge – Peter West

Long, long ago, at a time before God, or Gods, had arrived in people's minds, lived a being, an ordinary being, a little different to others of their number.

This child was wise, and those around them found value in this and were happy to work while the special one thought, a mutual arrangement that suited everyone.

Over time, the special one grew, thought, learned from community and travellers alike, a lifetime of days spent in thought and nights around the campfire, the place for all to relax and learn from each other when the end of each day came, for none were beyond their learning and wondering.

A good life, a rewarding life, a life that found high esteem, but, of course, all things must end.

After a very long life, the special one died! The community's inner circle knew not what they should do, but they recognised their obligation to ensure the passing on the special one's knowledge.

The 'circle' sent a message to other dwelling leaders and elders, asking what they should do? A very long delay ensued and more and more added to the list but, while all agreed that the special one's accumulated knowledge must not be lost, there was still no idea forthcoming.

Through the heat of summer and cold of winter, the body now, through natural processes, took on a waxy texture, not unlike cheese. Here they understood, was the answer to their dilemma, the community finally knew what to do!

People, wise leaders and shamen, gradually arrived, great numbers from every side, "the special one" was held in such high regard. They had journeyed from all directions and camped as they arrived and in order of their arrival.

After due ceremony, the head and brain, divided into small pieces, was given to the assembled, now throng, for consumption 'on the spot!' What better way could there be to absorb the power of knowledge and learning, while the rest was distributed, becoming 'relics' of our world's first genius?

From this wisdom comes an understanding that your view of an idea/concept/problem is dependent on the direction you approach it from and that each takes from it their concept of what is correct.

I'm having trouble with this concept myself but – Each person has their perspective, viewing from their distance and angle, not their point of view but their observation point.

If the special one faces North and you approach him from the North, he will always meet you face to face; and what the first of 'the come afters' received was the front, but most central part of the brain, likewise with the others. If you approach from the South, he will always lead you, and from East or West, he will always be beside you. Each, in turn, received their portion until, sadly, all was gone.

And so it is with ideas, it all depends on your direction of approach!

38 A good man – Robert Greener

Prompt: In life, he had been a good man...

In life, he had been a good man, but he supposed that was only his opinion anyway, and he didn't know if anyone else had noticed. He wasn't in the habit of broadcasting his thoughts and actions to all and sundry – the world of social media was not designed for him. Either way, moral relativity seemed to be the order of the day, probably always was even if the present crop of deities hadn't got the memo.

The older deities would have understood perfectly, just think of the way old Zeus used to conduct himself, jealous fits, carrying on with mortals and pulling children out of his head. Crazy stuff, is that what we aspire to?

Wonder what happened to the old bugger, he thought as he drifted off into what he imagined would be his final sleep, I suppose it will all be clear soon enough.

39 As Above So Below – Briar Noonan

Chapter 1: In the Beginning....

It was different to its environment in a way that made it aware of that single fact and no other. It did not know in what manner it was different, separated from, withdrawn from? It was only aware of its own being as a separate entity. The awareness was timeless and could not be measured for time did not exist, nor did space for both are artificial constructs yet to be conceived.

There arose within its being a need to know itself beyond its current perception. Was this need intrinsic to its own nature, something that came from its own being? Or manipulated from outside itself? It did not know and would not understand such a question or, indeed, the impulse to form the question itself, but it responded by extending its being into the need.

The call of its need became stronger and deep within itself there was an answering response, its own being which had been singular becoming reciprocal, a duality within its nature. Question and answer, impulse and response. Its evolution, which had begun so simply would take eons, in terms of unmeasured, unexistent and unknown time.

We will call the answer to its need, desire, perhaps aspiration, but it was more of a fulfilment once it became aware that it was not alone. The knowledge that it was not unique in its existence leant neither pleasure nor satisfaction for both were still experiences that were unknown to it.

Knowledge of its own existence and the existence of others that were similar led on to the next need which arose, the need to experience itself as a single entity and its purpose for being. It reached out to the others that it sensed in some indeterminate manner, by extending its newly forming will. There was no response but merely an increasing sense of its own solitary state which was not satisfactory anymore.

Having learnt that it was able to extend its will outwards from whatever its existence was, it extended it further to find something other than self. There was a sense of searching, reaching out until the sense changed and became altered having met a resistance which was all consuming. It had never experienced the sensations that flooded its being and had to learn how to catalogue them as it continued to evolve.

It was constrained, encapsulated, in a different plane of existence to that which it had known before whilst still retaining knowledge of the two states. It was as though a portion of its being was outside of itself and almost independent. The need arose again and with it the desire to learn about this new experience, to examine every facet of what it was sensing but it could only dimly feel what it was. The sense of feeling was not adequate for its needs and so it withdrew to ponder on what it had learnt.

When it again extended itself into experience its desire for increased sensitivity had responded to its own inner need and so the material which enclosed its perceptions gave back information not previously found. One such item of information was a sensation that felt heavy, completely different to its normal state which was the exact opposite, having no weight at all. Such a completely new experience satisfied it until, through no volition on its part, its will could no longer sense weight.

For something that could respond to its own inner needs and form a learning development, the experience of a happening that it was subjected to rather than forming, provided further scope for its development and an incentive to once again project its will into the density that was form.

The experience was the same, for it was the same experience and with its new found ability, it was aware of the fact and knew that it was capable of repeating as much as it wished, as long as the need was present. Repetition was not enough and so it extended its will with the need to experience something that was not the same, not a repeat. What ensued was similar but in some subtle manner it could ascertain that this was slightly different. There was the awareness of weight, that new thing that it knew, but there was a newness in the quality of it which was initially the same but as it concentrated upon it, the sensation altered, from one state to another. It had discovered something different from its own entire existence; it had discovered time, a thing which existed only in the new dimension to which it had reached out.

The new discovery prompted many separations of its being as it projected into the new dimension, into different forms of weight, of being encapsulated, and as its knowledge grew it was able to recognise a pattern. The contact at first felt strong, another new sensation which it had learnt, but with the passage of the peculiar nature of that plane, time, the strength diminished, the weight became more, until consciousness of its extension was returned and it became complete unto itself once again but now, with greater experience and knowledge gained from being in the other state.

Having exhausted all possibilities of the variety of such an experience, its inner need drove it to use its will in a different way. It attempted to extend the use of its will into not a singular unit but to a collection, a group, of them. Perhaps in that way, it would remain in some parts when others had come to an end. It learnt that this was the case and experienced what it now knew as an ending, death of some parts of its extended being, but the strongest part continued and it was only when that strongest part ended that its will withdrew.

The place that was different to itself, where it projected its will to, was in a dimension where time existed. It learnt that there was a pattern to existence there, a start, followed by being and, as it did in its own existence, a period when learning and evolution took place, before coming to an end and death. A death which required it to will itself into being in a different host, if its' desire for evolution continued as its driving motivation.

It had been accustomed to the sensation of weight and now also of time but its knowledge of its surroundings was limited to what it could feel and sense, until on one of its forays into the other existence, it inhabited something which sensed in a new way. It became aware of sight, as images, blurred and indistinct, flooded its being. Never having experienced anything like these new sensations it could not equate them with previously learnt knowledge and had to project into many different hosts before accepting them as a process which was used to acquaint the host body of the environment in which it temporarily existed.

A whole new way of being was explored and each time the new sense of sight became stronger because it had purposefully projected into organisms which were best developing this facility. It now knew and recognised other shapes which existed in its plane of experience and after a few of its hosts had come to an end by the agency of the new shapes, it drew the conclusion that not everything that existed in the mortal plane was aiding in its development. It tried to project into one of the different shapes but found that it was not comfortable with the vibration, there was a jarring sensation that was inimical to its being and in no way conducive to its continuing development.

It had noted that there was a sensation of movement in its vehicle, not threatening like the appearance of the different forms, but with a rhythm that was natural to this place and unthreatening, a natural part of the environment. There were fluctuations during this rhythm, a type of cyclic alteration of its ability to see and during the period when it was difficult to see there was a tendency to drift into a less aware state. Early, it had learnt that the host that it occupied had a method of extracting qualities from its surroundings which it needed to survive and this too, was of a cyclic nature.

Chapter 2: A new beginning

Another day with no definite purpose and nothing on the horizon except tidying the already neat bungalow and preparing a solitary meal. She was expecting no callers and it was still a week to go before the next village coffee morning, the only time that there was any interaction with others, unless there was a chance meeting with a neighbour when putting out the bins.

Fortunately Joan was happy with her enclosed existence and sufficiently self motivated to be always able to find an occupation for her busy hands, often accompanied by the television chattering away in the background. She particularly liked quiz shows as they did not require much watching, more listening really, which allowed her eyes to concentrate on the work in hand. She also believed that they stimulated her brain and often surprised herself by the range of knowledge that she seemed to possess, whilst at others she was appalled by suspicions of incipient senility.

The day stretched before her with only the usual milestones in sight when she was alerted to the fact that the postman had been by the clatter of the letterbox. The usual junk mail, which went immediately into the recycling bin, a statement from the bank letting her know that she was still solvent, barely, and a picture postcard from Istanbul that can only have been sent by one person, her grandson Luke. His gap year travels had begun a few weeks ago and she had missed his presence in her life, missed having him around the home which he shared with her during term time, his parents house being too far away from College.

After reading of his adventures, which seemed to revolve around finding a MacDonalds everywhere he visited, she took the card into the bedroom which had been his and stuck it on his pin board above the desk. She had to lean across the desk to reach and after lifting up her hand she saw its imprint in a thin layer of dust on top of the square black box underneath. Fetching a duster she sprayed and polished everything to within an inch of its life, grateful for something to fill the empty morning whilst being careful not to disturb all the wires and connections in Luke's arcane collection of gadgets.

Sitting on his bed she looked at the swivel chair where he used to sit for hours playing his games, his earphones with the little microphone attached to them sat forlornly on top of the black box and she remembered all the times that she had tried to get his attention at mealtimes only for him to say,

"Just a minute Gran, I can't leave it now or I will be killed!"

She had felt like replying that she would kill him herself, if his food got cold, but of course, she never did. Later he would sometimes tell her of the situation he, or rather his character, had been in, of how much his party were depending upon him in a difficult story line and how he would lose XP if he died!

He had tried to explain the concept of XP and other components of the fictional world that he inhabited when wearing those headphones and shouting into the microphone, but most of it had met with the usual,

"That's nice dear" from Joan

The room felt as empty as her life and no amount of self admonishment could keep the loneliness at bay. Telling herself that she was pleased that he was having such a grand adventure and assuring herself that it 'would be the making of him' did not bring much comfort as her eyes dwelt on the reminders of what was lost. With a slight creak in her knees she levered herself off the bed and went to sit in his chair, just to feel a little closer to him and picking up the headset she twiddled the small microphone around and around as she pictured his remembered image shouting into it.

Strangely, it almost retained an aroma of his smell, not unpleasant because he was a clean boy, but evocative of his personal scent. She put it on, settling the cushioned ear pads snugly around her ears and positioning the microphone in front of her mouth, just as she had seen Luke do before he pushed the button on the black box. Without any conscious volition, Joan reached out her hand and did the same, jumping back in alarm as the fanfare of music assailed her ears and the screen in front of her lit up with a bright green glow. After that initial shock she was about to push the button again, hoping that she had not broken anything, when the picture on the screen changed to show what looked like a selection of different game boxes, one of which was highlighted and she recognised the name as being Luke's favourite, he had told her about it often enough!

From familiarity with choosing her television programmes Joan knew that it was waiting for her to choose something from the selection offered and there was an internal struggle with herself about what she should do. Obviously, she should turn off the box, replace the headphones on top and leave the room in peace, after all, the oven was in need of a good clean.

Her hands appeared to be developing a will of their own for instead of exiting and pulling on the bright yellow Marigolds, they were reaching out for the gadget that Luke always held in his hands when playing his games. His fingers used to fly across the various buttons and triggers and Joan wondered how on earth he remembered what they all did. Strange the way in which young people seemed to be born with an aptitude for pressing buttons, she reflected, remembering the speed with which he sent texts to his friends from his mobile phone. It took her half the morning, or so it seemed, to send a text to her friend Marjorie, and even then half the letters were wrong.

The screen still patiently showed the same selection of games as she held the gadget which bore little resemblance to her television controller. Admittedly, there were buttons which she could understand so she decided to start with them. A,

B, Y and X, what sort of strange alphabet was that, she asked herself? With a sense of trepidation she pressed the A, it seemed to be the place to start, the first letter of the alphabet.

There was another, smaller fanfare of music, and the picture changed to show a scene from some sort of strange world before lots of different images telling her who had made the game, a little like the credits before a film, Joan thought. The screen then asked her if she wanted to Resume or Start a New Game. Well, she thought, I cannot resume Luke's game and I really should turn it off before I do any damage but it was such a treat to be doing something different from the usual humdrum routine that she did not want to stop.

Joan noticed that of the two questions on the screen, one of them, the Resume one was highlighted as the game selection one had been earlier. Reasoning that pressing A had selected that particular game Joan reasoned that pressing A again would select Resume but there was no way to highlight New Game. Perhaps if she pressed B or one of the other two letters? Nothing happened. Her heart rate increased as she tentatively pressed the buttons on the front of the gadget, carefully avoiding the two lever things which stuck up on the top. Again nothing happened until she was about to give up the whole experiment and she inadvertently moved one of the mushroom shaped levers as she went to put the control gadget down. The highlight now surrounded the words New Game! Now, she knew, it was safe to press the A button.

40 Had they intended... – Peter West

Had they intended me to leave, or was it that I escaped, all I knew was that I had to get away. Too grim to bear any longer, and I daren't look at what they'd done.

The only choice was out into the blazing sun and gain distance to, somehow, escape across the dunes, miles and miles of gruelling heat and sand. Some say travel by night, but how, dig in like the few desert animals? I did find it better with my body covered by sand and my ragged blood-stained shirt over my head and face to keep the ever-invasive sand from my eyes and ears.

I even slept for a short while, and the sand was surprisingly kind to my wounds, absorbent and reasonably sterile; things could have been so much worse.

As darkness fell, it was time to move or, at least, struggle to move, and at last, a rocky outcrop and the chance of some proper shelter but still nothing more. I drift into a half-sleeping state and, at some stage, wake to hear faint sounds. I haven't looked at my surroundings' just grateful that the rock warms me as it gives back the heat that pounded it during the day. I get up to explore and stagger around to, eventually, find a split in the rock where the sound is a little louder.

Once inside, it's a split or fissure but seemingly worn by the passage of many. I move forward, the worn floor slopes gently downward, and the sound, the sound of running water, gets a little louder as I make my way forward through the narrow fissure. I suddenly realise where I must be, but it's water, I must get to it. Down and down, ever nearer, until I see water, somehow, inexplicably, the way is lit by torches fixed into, seemingly, holes chiselled into the rock and there is light enough to see the way to the water's edge and to the other side.

Down to the water, no boatman in-sight! I check as best I can and then down to the water to drink at last. It's good, so refreshing, but I need to rest before I can cross. A niche in the rock a little way back gives me safety and enough comfort to sleep just a little, before I find myself in the water swimming for all I'm worth, 'can't wait for the boatman; he might never come for me!

Gasping, half drowning, I feel rocks against my body; I've reached the other side, I drag myself out, hands and knees bloodied, the least of my worries. I settle down to rest again but notice where I've come from, the black slithering dangers that could have been my end.

And then I awake, two black nurses standing over me – in ITU. Somehow!

Holy Days and Holy Thoughts

41 A Story for Imbolc – Briar Noonan

How long ago was it, that Samhuinn when I had my first 'weird experience'? one of a handful which have come to me and been held lightly at the back of my mind, to be taken out and wondered at only years after the event.

We had gathered in the late afternoon of a cold dreary day, hopeful that the skies would clear in time for the open-air ritual scheduled for dusk, one of the two magical times; dawn and dusk, a time of day when there is a fragile balance between dark and light. As the wind and increasingly heavy rain battered at windows and doors it was reluctantly accepted that the evening's celebration of the end of the Celtic year would need to be held indoors for it was even worse than the night of the autumn equinox when a small, foolhardy group of druids had balanced on narrow beams across the muddy woodland floor evoking the spirit of balance in a changing world. This time we capitulated to the forces of nature and gathered in the warmer, and drier, glass walled conservatory.

It was fortunate that our host had recently extended his property and that the area was large enough to hold a dozen or so with ease, it was even more fortunate that the wall connecting the conservatory to the house held a nicely roaring wood fire. This, and the candles, gave sufficient light as the circle was cast and the ceremony began. During the central part we were each directed to find a solitary position within the room, to conduct our personal meditation on the year which was just ending and in doing so, to select those things which were not needed on the journey into the dark time of the year between Samhuinn and the Winter Solstice. All knew that there would be an opportunity later in the ceremony to symbolically 'give away' these things to the Cailliacht, the crone Goddess of Winter.

Finding a comfortable perch I addressed myself to the task in hand, sinking easily into a reverie as I looked through the window at the dark night raging outside. The year since my first initiation last Samhuinn had passed well, there were many happy memories and the earlier hardship of finding myself living alone and in a new job had become easier making it possible to appreciate the blessings I had received, indeed, I was hard put to squeeze out a few tears or think of anything which needed to be relinquished. Perhaps it was for that reason that I became so interested in what I discerned in the dark window in front of me, for a picture had slowly formed. Initially I assumed that what I saw was a reflection of the room behind me, for the darkness beyond the glass had the effect of making the window more like a mirror than clear glass. There were certainly lights which I ascribed to the candles behind, but no, it was more than that.

The picture which was building was of a path which led between the tree trunks of a forest, not very wide, and narrowing, as it stretched before my gaze away into the gloom. The intriguing thing was that the path seemed lit from within and the light spilled upwards against the boles of the trees on either side, whilst away in the far distance of the dark forest I could see a single, bright light burning steadily. Rubbing my eyes I tried in vain to return to my introspection. It was no use, for the picture remained on my inner vision. Again I opened my eyes, resolved that it was merely a combination of my imagination and the reflection of the room behind me, I turned around and checked before looking once more into the glass. It was still there, stronger than ever and so I had no choice but to accept it.

Later, in my interaction with the Cailliacht I had nothing to cast away but I did ask if I might walk the path which I had seen, to which the Crone replied that I was already on it.

Mildly interesting you might say, but surely this rambling epic is entitled a story for Imbolc,and not Samhuinn? Fast forward eight or nine years.

It is now Imbolc and the snow is falling softly on a darkened night in the Wyre Forest. We are a larger group than that long ago night of Samhuinn but still small enough to have achieved a warm bonding in the few days that we have spent together in the cosy yurt, piling wood into the wood burning stove and sleeping side by side on the carpeted floor, sharing stories and chanting softly by the light of kerosene lanterns and candles. Earlier today one of our number had prepared a candle lit labyrinth and we are all bubbling with eagerness to walk it by the light of the moon, as we sort through the jumble of boots and wellingtons by the door to the yurt. (Why do so many people bring identical green wellies to camp?) Eventually finding a pair which fit and hoping that they really are mine I fasten up my warm padded jacket, don my lovely black ski hat with ear flaps,(which makes me look like Cardinal Wolsley, my friend reliably informs me), I step out into the clear, chill air.

Just outside the yurt the frozen ground is covered with straw which squelches slightly as we mill around, it was just such milling which caused the quagmire in the first place it occurs to me, but eventually we all trail off up the slight hill towards the scheduled start of the walking meditation. Many pause as they pass the altar to Brigid, the Goddess honoured at this time of year, and some light a fresh candle or admire the gentle snowdrops which abound in this place, before passing on with a heightened sense of reverence.

Having dawdled overlong I am towards the back of the group as we are marshalled into a double line by Daru, who sends people off on the path at slight intervals. It would be easy to pass the time in friendly banter with him and others as I wait but somehow it just doesn't seem appropriate in this time and space, so I look instead at the arching stars above me. at the moon and the silvery glow which seems to permeate everything as the moonbeams strike the frost rimed branches of the trees. Even my breath, which plumes all around me, is fascinating to my teary gaze as the cold forces warm teardrops into frozen eyes.

At last I am at the front and ready to make my own personal journey down the track and into the forest. Drawing my attention to the task in hand I look before me to where Daru indicates the start of the Labyrinth, and the last few years of my life fall away. Again I am back on that cold, wet, autumn night of Samhuinn, for before me is the vista that I last saw then. The pathway is lit by lights on either side, simple really, just brown paper bags with a trowel full of cold earth in the bottom and a tea light placed on top, the sides forming a shelter from the wind but allowing sufficient light through so that they become magical lights, floating in the blackness. As, once before, I watch the light spilling upwards from each rustic lantern and splaying against the boles of the darkened trees, their branches invisible in the night sky above. Eventually, I start to breathe again and conscious of others pressing forward behind me I place one hesitant foot before the other and make my way down the lighted path.

Surely this cannot be happening my strangled voice murmurs, there must be some difference, I think, as I gaze towards the culmination of the journey for the single, bright shining light which I fear will not be there. But no, it is there and as I head towards it I already know in my heart what I will find.

Not a candle but a fire, only a small one but built beside the small pool and adjacent to the single standing stone which marks the centre of the small ceremonial grove, here in the ancient lands of the Cornovii tribe. The memories come flooding back as I sink onto a warm stone at the side of the fire.

Seasonal celebrations of the wheel of the year held within this space. Initiations, a few Bardic ones and my own Ovate one a few years ago, but, more recently, my final Druid grade initiation, here on this very spot only last night. I re-live the rite, the nervousness as I was questioned and examined, the sweetness of the harp played by a Scandinavian Druid I had never met previously, the otherworld quality which had invaded my blindfolded senses, the warmth of friendship and the welcoming hugs once it was all over.

Sitting here for hours as the fire slowly burns down and people come and go among the trees behind me, none of them intruding on my introspection for all recognise my need to be alone, I wonder what it all means. Has everything I have done and learnt during the last few years been pre-ordained and was my journey so far completely out of my hands? am I merely a puppet carrying out a plan which I have no understanding of? Are there loops in time which allow us sometimes to see our own future?

As I write this little story I am still not really sure, all I can be sure of is that I am still on that path and still hoping to reach that greater light at the end of it.

42 Christmas Remembered – Maggie Bannister

My childhood was unusual. The eldest of five, I had responsibility thrust on me at an early age, and often helped in the kitchen, doing the chores and collecting my siblings at mealtimes, even when that meant a visit to the local park to find my brother and the family dog.

But Christmas was different. At Christmas my mother took over. We had very little money, even though we lived in a big house. My mother saved little treats for us all year, hiding pencils, colouring books, tiny parcels of brightly-wrapped chocolate squares, chocolate umbrellas, little toys, and anything she could find to make the christmas stocking the highlight of our year. I never knew where she hid all these things, and they were her personal choice for us all. There was always one thing which was different for each of us, and she knew exactly what we would like. We never asked for anything. We knew there was very little money. We didn't expect anything. I think we did make lists but certainly didn't think it mattered. They were written on scraps of paper and put in the fireplace where they would burn with the next fire.

On Christmas Eve a huge tree would arrive in the house, on which my mother draped a set of lights, checking every bulb. Then it was down to us. We children decorated it with well-worn baubles, home-made decorations, and the little strands of sparkly tinsel which littered the carpet within hours. The whole house would be draped with paper chains, carefully saved from the previous year. Every room had long strips of crepe paper taped to the ceiling and twisted and fixed to the corners of the room, or plaited and placed in any spare space. We decorated everywhere, even our bedrooms. Sometimes our grandparents would be there to supervise, tidy up, help reach the bits of ceiling which even standing on the back of the sofa we couldn't reach.

In the hallway a well-worn box would appear. Inside was a wooden stable with a straw roof, a bundle of straw, and the nativity figures, which we arranged and carefully put in place. I remember making a small star to add to the scene. It was all carefully placed on the big wooden chest in the hall.

In the church, reached directly through corridors, Mr. Collett the churchwarden was at work making another nativity scene. There was a doorway in the church which at one time led into our back garden, but was used Christmas and Easter to make beautiful constructions. The Christmas one was another nativity scene, filling the width of the doorway, with what I thought were beautiful figures. He allowed us to watch him, as over several days the cave and its surrounding garden would be lovingly constructed behind the door, only to be revealed on Christmas Eve when the doors were opened and the baby Jesus would be placed in the stable.

Back in the house we went to bed with feelings of excitement and expectation. Each of us laid one of Mum's old stockings across the foot of the bed.
Next morning when we woke, the first thing we

felt was the weight of that stocking, crammed with little treats. it's amazing how much you can fit in an 'American Tan' stocking. Always an orange in the stocking's toe to eat at the end, and we knew that that orange was special too. Fruit was expensive, and Mum rarely ate any, saving it for her children. She had an arrangement with the local greengrocer whereby he gave her Seville oranges each year, and she provided him with marmalade in return, and I think he was generous with the fruit and vegetables when she shopped there.

We would open our stockings with glee, and then after breakfast it was time for church, while Mum slaved over the coal-fuelled Aga.

Christmas dinner was the biggest meal of the year. We always had extra people for lunch. Grandparents, usually, but also people who lived alone or had no family who would be invited to join us. An extra table would be laid and joined to the main table. At Christmas this was our table. The children's table. The adults sat at the main table and once we had our plates piled high with delicious food, and Grace had been said. the feast began. Sprouts (my favourite), bread sauce spiced with cloves and peppercorns, chunks of soft onion and creamy bread and so good on sprouts! Big crunchy roast potatoes, meltingly soft in the middle, mounds of stuffing, and crunchy pigs in blankets. And a slice of turkey. All eaten with freshly made English mustard that made you want to sneeze, and proper gravy.

The adults had a glass of wine and we all wore hats from the crackers, guessed the answers to the terrible jokes and laughed at the cheap plastic toys and puzzles.

Eventually the Christmas pudding came in flaming and then mum would carefully cut it so we all had a sixpence in our slice. And the trifle – proper trifle with real blancmange plenty of sherry, real fruit and no jelly.

Still no presents unwrapped though. They had to wait until the washing up was finished. And The Presents warrant a whole chapter to themselves!

43 Mother Christmas – Patrissia Cuberos

My mother was larger than life in more than one sense. To me, as a tiny five year-old, she seemed as big as an elephant or a whale. Of course, my own size and the imaginary size of those animals had nothing to do with reality. For today standards of obesity my mother was just a typical apple, whose middle would have happily won a competition with Father Christmas. But instead of the Ho Ho Ho, what shook her belly with mirth, were her own, often bawdy jokes.

But there was another thing for which she would have won a contest with Father Christmas: it was, her Christmas spirit.

When we talk about someone being 'the soul of the party' I often think that the only person I know who would deserve that qualification, was my mother.

For me, she invented Christmas; when she died, the spirit of Christmas died in my family.

Christmas evening at home was a time of light; not the light of candles or Christmas lights, but the light of my mother, running around, for once cheerful and never crossed – she used to be very bad tempered and prone to tantrums that made our lives at other times, a bit miserable.

I was frightened of my mum... except around Christmas.

She started the celebrations by organizing a paseo with piquete – a picnic in the countryside, on the first weekend of December, with large saucepans containing two chickens, salted

potatoes, guacamole, chilli, sauce and even rice.
This particular paseo was our opportunity to
collect moss, lichens and in general to disrobe the
mountains on the outskirts of Bogota, from a
good deal of their natural beauty, in order to
transfer them to our pesebre or nativity scene
populated by people, animals, plants and
buildings all sizes, from lilliputians to
Brobdingnagians, and all regions and
architectonical styles, from Israel in the first
century, to the New York of the fifties.

I don't know how my mother managed to
purchase, wrap, and more importantly hide the
dozens of presents she bought, nearly single
handed for her children, grand-children,
husbands and wives, until Christmas evening at
midnight, when 'miraculously', a baby Jesus big
enough to swallow his father whole, with turban
and cane to boot, appeared in his crib.

We always had as many of our large family
around for the traditional Christmas evening
meal, and it was one of the handful of special
occasions every year when we got to taste the
legendary 'mother's touch in the kitchen. Her
buñuelos – traditional Christmas cornflower,
fresh cheese and egg balls, fried and served
doused with light syrup, were awaited, coveted
and devoured by the fifty or so guests, She would
have spent at least 4 or 5 hours on her feet
preparing them, even though she suffered
standing for long on semi-high heels, and with
her weight.

But she never complained and the memory of those Christmases still fills my years with light, cheer and love.

Gracias, madrecita.

44 The Presents – Maggie Bannister

Oh my goodness me, the Presents. I don't even
really remember what they contained, apart from
a few unfortunate things my dear mother gave
me. It was the present -opening ritual that I shall
never forget. By this time it was well after 3 pm.
The meal had been eaten, and the washing up
finished, so that my mother could finally relax.
My father was finished for the day and was by
now only wanting to sit down with the dog and
close his eyes.

I don't know why there were so many presents
under the tree, or where they all came from. But
with a family with 5 children, 4 grandparents,
and various ladies and aunts who gave presents,
once we all sat down there was hardly room to
move in the increasingly warm room, the fire
crackling in the grate and a huge pile of coal in
the scuttle. Until I was about 12 at least, we had
no central heating and there were fires in various
stages of safety all-round the house in the winter,
from the gas fire in our bedroom which had been
condemned by the gas board, but still connected
so we lit it and piled up the broken elements
precariously like a dangerous game of Jenga,
completely ignorant of any danger. Or the oil
heaters which were moved around the house
which were from some ancient time when it was
normal to do so. Why the house hadn't gone up
in flames I have no idea. The fire in the lounge
usually only seemed to warm about a yard in
front of it, but at Christmas time the number of
people in the room kept us all warm.

First of all, the presents were divided up, and passed round unopened until everyone had a pile of brightly wrapped parcels with their names on in front of them. How we waited I don't know, but this was the ritual, and this is what we did every year. Then, starting with the youngest, we would unwrap one present at a time while everyone watched until it had been admired and passed round for everyone to see. And so on. Once the oldest in the room had unwrapped one present, it was the youngest's turn again and so on until every present had been opened. The wrapping paper would be put in a separate bag, to be smoothed and folded and kept for next year. Meanwhile my grandfather would write on a piece of paper the details of the present, who it was for, who it was from, and what it was, so that on Boxing Day we could all write our Thank-you letters without any mistakes or omissions. It all sounds very orderly but it really wasn't. We are a noisy family when we all get together and everyone talks at once. I remember that chaos with a mixture of affection and incredulity. If anyone was feeling cross or sad, there was no point because no one would notice, and Mum always kept everyone's sprits up.

The present unwrapping ceremony went on for hours until everyone had their presents, everyone had seen them, and we had started on the chocolates or the big bowl of nuts, whose shells littered the fireplace and the floor.

There was one exception to the participation in this careful ritual: my father, who by this time was exhausted with Christmas preparations, Christmas Services, and talking to people. My dad was gregarious but I think he was actually quite introvert, so that being in company exhausted him. When it was his turn to open a present, he would find the two he wanted – a book and a bag of liquorice allsorts, open them and be perfectly content to ignore the chaos around him while he read. It didn't matter what it was. He was happy with anything from the Beano Annual to a book of poetry, and everything in between. He would immediately open the book and start it, and eating the liquorice allsorts which were shared with the dog, leading to unfortunate circumstances later on. He then was blissfuly unaware of the chaos around him, only coming to when it was his turn to open yet another parcel of socks or handkerchiefs.

His mother, our Grandma, was always with us for Christmas. She loved opening her presents, which always seemed to be highly scented bathsalts, or those soaps that looked and smelled like lemons. Or a bottle of her favourite scent, called 4711. As she got older she would keep all these 'smellies' as she called them in a drawer in her bedroom, and we discovered later on that she would run a bath for herself every week, and fill it with the scented bathsalts, but because of her 'bad knees' she couldn't actually get into the bath, and she didn't want people to realise that, so she ran the baths anyway. But Grandma's 'smellies' would be passed round for everyone to sample, and I remember wondering why the scent didn't wear off, with all of us having a sniff.

The most interesting, and sometimes bizarre, presents were sent from my Dad's cousin and aunt in Nova Scotia. Sometime before Christmas, a well wrapped parcel would arrive from Canada. In it were wrapped presents for us, and something extra, often a novelty-shaped candle, the idea of which hadn't yet reached the UK shops, so a candle shaped like a Christmas Tree, or Snowman, or Santa, would sometimes grace the tea table on Boxing day. One year it was a box of beautiful candied fruits. The parcel would arrive with a customs label attached detailling the contents, which my mother insisted she had torn off without reading, so that it would be as much a surprise for her on Christmas Day. I'm sure that's absolutely true. Mum was the master of self control.

They did send odd presents though. One year we all got two crocodile clips linked with a small chain. Cardigan clips apparently. Whoever knew such things existed. They caused much hilarity and speculation on opening. Or the year they sent us all (girls, anyway) a pair huge nylon knickers each. Dad always got a book from Canada. I remember the year they sent my dad a book of poems by a Canadian poet called Leonard Cohen. When he turned those poems into songs and Dad bought the LP, we learned the songs and wrote the chords over the words in the poetry book. I don't know what happened to that book but if only it had been saved from my father, who had no concept of possession, and gave most things away without a second thought.

The point of the presents wasn't what they contained. They were tiny things. Often hand-knitted jumpers or clothes we needed. Sometimes there was a board game (ready for Boxing Day) or variety packs of sweets and chocolates. But the ritual of it all and watching other people's faces as they carefully unwrapped the parcels was what gave me joy. It still does. I love surprises. I can't see the point of knowing what you are getting, but I'm sure that this stems from the gifts being inexpensive. The idea that someone has taken the trouble to think about their friends and loved ones, chosen a gift and wrapped it up for them, no matter how small, is such a generous and thoughtful mark of love, it makes me happy.

I can't remember eating any more on Christmas Day. Maybe turkey and mustard sandwiches for supper.

I think it was mostly saved for Boxing Day, which was when The Relatives came, and the Tongue was unearthed from the pantry.

45 A Druid Christmas – Briar Noonan

Do Druids celebrate Christmas? This is one of the questions I am sometimes asked. The short answer is yes, of course we do, in much the same way that other non-Christian people in this country and around the world do. It has become so much a civil festival that very often the true meaning of the time of year is swamped under a mass of tinsel and festive food.

Getting away from the social aspects and turning to the spiritual side of the darkest month of the year, Druids and other Pagans generally attach more importance to the Winter Solstice and the celebration of Yule, in fact it is vitally important in terms of the turning of the wheel of the year. Most celebrate with a ritual which features the extinguishing of all light to symbolise the shortest day of the year, a time when the sun is as far away from earth as it ever goes, before we commence our journey of return. After a period of reflection, a single light is kindled and the return of the Mabon is celebrated.

The Mabon is the child of Light and there are very obvious parallels with the birth of Christ which is probably one of the reasons why this time of year was chosen by the Christian church as the birth date of Jesus of Nazareth. Symbolically the light has returned and will grow in strength throughout the next six months in the same manner that a child grows from the day of its birth.

One of my lasting memories of this time of year took place during the Winter Solstice gathering of the Order of Bards, Ovates and Druids in Glastonbury. A ritual journey was staged to connect with the mystical search for the Mabon at this time of year. For those who have never experienced this type of event I would like to briefly explain the concept.

Most people are familiar with the inner journeys which are made in imagination, where someone will read a script detailing what and who the traveller will meet along the way whilst the rest of the participants sit in a meditative state, often in a darkened room. Descriptions will vary and often they will be quite broad to allow the traveller's own psyche to fill in the gaps and to make realisations which is the purpose of the whole thing, in the majority of instances.

In a ritual journey the participant walks through the stages physically, not just in imagination. Along the way there are generally locations where situations are set up with individuals facilitating them who have taken on the personae of whoever they are meant to be and with whom, the celebrant will interact. Samhain (Halloween) is a popular time for this type of facilitated, interactive, ritual drama.

Druidry is rich in myth and legend, working closely with the land, the animal and the plant kingdoms. On the journey in question, which was held in Chalice Wells gardens after closing time, the participants went to various locations to question at each a facilitator who had 'become' one of the mystical creatures from legend with the aid of costume, makeup and masks. There was an Owl, perched up in a tree hooting morosely to the night sky, a wise old Eagle in a feathered head dress/mask (which it had taken me weeks to make), a Stag, again in a fabulous horned head dress and finally the famous Salmon of Wisdom who had feasted on the magic hazelnuts floating in the pool in the west. This last was a disembodied voice from the location designated as the pool of wisdom.

It is standard, in this type of journey that the early stages of the quest do not contain the answers that one is seeking but merely pass the seeker on to the next stage and so, the three earlier creatures had not known where the Mabon had been born although they knew of the return of the light and were therefore able to direct us on to the next creature that was even wiser than themselves, and who we therefore needed to question.

The night was crisp and clear, it was cold but we were prepared and well wrapped in winter cloaks and woollen mittens as we journeyed throughout the darkened gardens. The sound of water was ever present from the wells as we journeyed in silence to our next destination. As we reached the summit on the gentle rise which led to the location of the Salmon of Wisdom the night sky was arched across us, shining with the radiant light of a full moon and stars. it was very easy to identify, in a small way, with those wise men 2,000 years ago who had undertaken their own similar quest.

My Atheist, lapsed Catholic, husband had reluctantly joined in the journey and I was surprised after it was over to hear him say how profound an effect it had wreaked upon him, not an instant conversion, but certainly, food for thought.

Perhaps the story is not as important as the journey and the desire to connect with the re-birth of the light. Something deep within our being calls to the light at the time of deepest darkness and the form that our call takes is purely that, just a form that embodies and expresses a very basic human need.

Dion Fortune said that all the gods are one God and all goddesses are one Goddess, I would obviously agree and go further, by saying that all stories are expressing the same concept – a human search for understanding, however it is expressed, it is the search and the intent which can lead to the personal insight of the meaning of it all.

46 An angel's breath can drift ever forward – Maggie Bannister

Gathering her helpers, her homecoming invites immense joy.

Knowing limitless love, the morning meets night,

opening the portal's radiance so slightly,

so tenderly

that the traces touched unify the Universe.

Unknown, undiscovered voices weave wonderful whimsical webs.

Xmas -

yesterday's youth -

your yonder zenith.

Meet the Authors

Maggie Bannister

Maggie was born in London and studied law at Leicester. Although she did not pursue a legal career, she used her sharp legal mind and concise writing skills to help many in the voluntary sector and community groups.

When Covid came, many of her choir friends found a place for their creative outlets in the new Wordthreads writing group. Maggie suddenly found an ability and love of writing - and in surprisingly abstract subjects, such as pigeons, or potatoes (!) and latterly in beautiful deep-felt poems about her family.

Sadly, Maggie passed away as we were putting the finishing touches to Pigeon Tales, our poetry collection and is probably reading it from up there, together with this title, both homage to her wit and imagination.

Patrissia Cuberos

Patrissia used to be always late. Blame her Colombian upbringing. So, she only arrived at the magical world of words- her greatest passion - in her mid-forties after living the drama of Opera and Tango on stage and life.

She breakfasts with a good dose of optimism and a bowl of fruit, nuts and yoghurt. Depending on wallet, waistline and weather, she likes lemon drizzle cake or ice cream for tea. She dreams of becoming a successful writer and pianist by eighty and an Artist/Fashion designer by ninety. That's optimism for you!

Author of ThePhysics of Passion Trilogy

Janet Cupit

Janet has always loved a good story. Her father used to make up bedtime stories for her and her sister about Mrs Goose's school , accompanied by his own illustrations. It is a joy to her that our rich literary legacy is there to be embraced and enjoyed by all generations. The support and encouragement of the Wordthreads group has helped her to fulfil a dream.

Robert Greener

Robert stumbled into writing after too many years of professional reports that failed to change the world; he can't think why he waited so long. He was guided into Wordthreads by the wonderful people he met during the re-launching of his choir-singing career. He is currently experimenting with Science Fiction and Fantasy with a side-line in Historical Fiction, and just generally having fun with words..

Briar Noonan

Briar has wide ranging interests, writing being one of them. Most interests are textile related from knitting and crochet to spinning and weaving and beyond that to combining multiple disciplines and creating wearable art....she is a dressmaker by trade. Underlying all of her leisure activities she is a Druid and a student of Kabbalah maintaining a deep interest in spiritual development.

Anila Syed

Anila Syed's love of short stories stems from the fiction of Wells, Clarke and Asimov among others. Although her career has led her to neuroscience, she has found a home with the WordThreads Authors, and loves to read and write alongside them.

Author of Prompted

Peter the Rascal! (West)

How did Peter, in his seventies, end up in a writing group? He doesn't think his life's been any more unusual than others; isn't there some quirk in everyone's life?

From age thirty-something, Morris dance was his thing. Then, at sixtyish, he joined Songthreads, stayed at least twelve years, and started an "a Capella trio" along the way. Finally, he became interested in trying to write songs, and Wordthreads brought him to this point.

Chris Westwood-Marshall

The pen is mightier than the sword. I passionately believe the world we humans have set up doesn't work and there has to be better way of interacting with this beautiful Earth which would 'carry on seamlessly without us' given the chance. I have always written but did not share those words until Lockdown. I loved the space and time to really think and also Zoom.

Printed in Great Britain
by Amazon

36369469R00145